700033061886

D1639694

The Meeker Massacre

THE
MEEKER
MASSACRE

WAYNE D. OVERHOLSER
AND LEWIS B. PATTEN

SAGEBRUSH
Large Print Westerns

First published in Great Britain by ISIS Publishing Ltd.
First published in the United States by Crowles

Published in Large Print 2010 by ISIS Publishing Ltd.,
7 Centremead, Osney Mead, Oxford OX2 0ES
United Kingdom
by arrangement with
Golden West Literary Agency

British Library Cataloguing in Publication Data
Overholser, Wayne D., 1906–1996.
    The Meeker massacre.
    1. Meeker, Nathan Cook, 1814–1879 - - Fiction.
    2. Ute Indians - - Wars, 1879 - - Fiction.
    3. Western stories.
    4. Large type books.
    I. Title II. Patten, Lewis B.
    813.5'2–dc22

ISBN 978–0–7531–8524–7 (hb)

Printed and bound in Great Britain by
T. J. International Ltd., Padstow, Cornwall

INTRODUCTION

In the fall of 1879, the dispute between the stubborn Ute Indians at White River Indian Agency, in northwestern Colorado, and their equally stubborn agent, Nathan C. Meeker, exploded into violence. Troops under Major T. T. Thornburgh were dispatched to Meeker's aid, but they were attacked by the Utes as they crossed the reservation boundary. It was two weeks before a relief force under Colonel Wesley Merritt could reach the agency. They found the agency buildings burned, the agency personnel slain, the women kidnapped by the Utes.

This "Ute War," as it was called in the newspapers of the time, climaxed years of broken promises, graft, and bungling in the government's handling of Indian affairs. But more significantly, it was the inevitable consequence of a collision between two vastly different cultures, that of the nomadic Utes, who were hunters and fighters, and that of the land-hungry whites, whose nation was expanding westward like a tide across the Indian lands. Though the bloodshed was tragic, it was welcomed by many whites because it led to displacement of the Utes and the opening of their lands to settlement.

Nathan Meeker, a good man who loved and wished to benefit the Utes and ended up peevishly trying to force his will upon them, was caught in the middle, along with his family and other agency employees.

This is the story of that tragic "Ute War" of 1879.

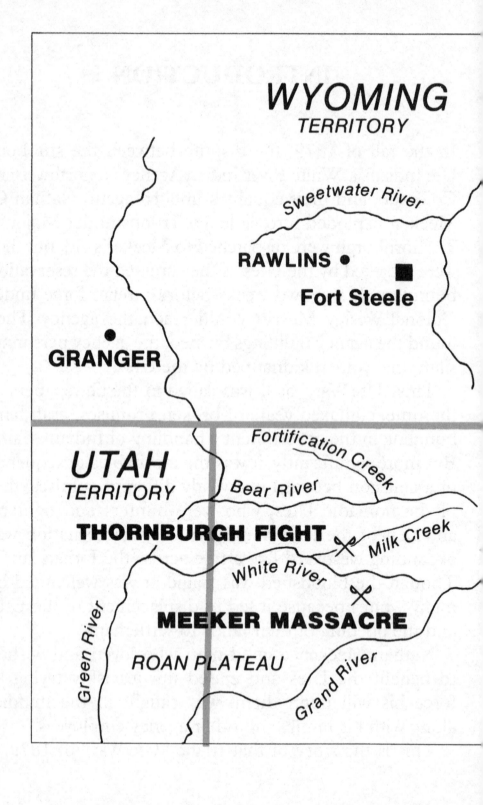

CHAPTER
ONE

Dave Madden stared out across the wide White River valley, looking eastward from the Indian Agency buildings. He could see Shad Price and his team just coming out from behind the trees that hid part of the horse pasture he was plowing. Beyond Price and his plow Dave could see the smoke coming from the Ute hide lodges, but he saw no Indians.

He put a halter on one of the big workhorses in the corral, and led the docile animal out, closing the gate carefully behind him. Holding the lunch bucket he had been told to take to Price, he vaulted to the horse's bare back.

Dave drummed his heels against the sides of his mount and the big animal broke into a jolting, awkward trot. Dave bounced up and down, but he balanced himself easily, holding the lard-pail lunch bucket away from his leg so it wouldn't hit him with every bounce.

He liked Shad Price. He also liked Price's young wife, Flora Ellen, and their two little children. He'd had the shivers this morning when he'd heard Nathan Meeker, the Indian agent, tell Price to hitch a team to the plow and go out and turn the sod in the big horse pasture east of the agency buildings.

Meeker had been warned by the Indians that there would be trouble if he plowed up any more of their horse pasture. But then, they had also warned him about plowing up their race-track and he had plowed it anyway. They hadn't followed up their threats. Maybe they wouldn't do anything about this, either.

Dave grinned ruefully. Why, then, was he so doggoned scared? Why had he tried so hard to think up an excuse for refusing to take Shad's lunch out to him?

He left the hard-packed dirt road about a quarter of a mile from the buildings and followed the trail of Shad's team and plow through a gate and along a narrow lane to the river bottom. He could see Price turning the corner up by the road and heading toward the agency.

Price had plowed only a narrow strip around the horse pasture since starting this morning. But the pasture was pretty large. Meeker had said it contained around two hundred acres.

Shad Price walked with the lines around his neck, holding the plow handles in his big, callused hands. Plowing sod wasn't easy work. Dave had done enough of it to know how the plow could jerk a man around.

He reached the near corner of the horse pasture. As he slid from the horse's back, he cast another uneasy glance in the direction of the Ute lodges. Then he sat down to wait for Price.

The feeling of trouble in the air wasn't exactly new to Dave. He had sensed it at the agency when he arrived several weeks ago, but it had been steadily getting worse. Even Dave, who was only seventeen, noticed the change. He could also see the growing irritability in Meeker, and the helplessness.

Dave had never been away from home very much before. He guessed he wouldn't be here now if his folks hadn't admired and trusted Meeker, who had been one of the founders of the Greeley, Colorado, cooperative agricultural settlement. When Meeker had asked Dave to hire on to help out at the agency, Mr. and Mrs. Madden had given their consent. But they wouldn't have, Dave knew, if Meeker had said trouble was building up over here.

A sound in the river bottom near the Indian lodges made Dave start violently. He stared uneasily into the thick underbrush in that direction. He didn't see anything alarming, or hear anything after that first sharp sound, which must have come from the snapping of a dry branch. Perhaps an Indian pony was working his way through the willows to the water.

Dave glanced out into the horse pasture again and saw that Price had turned the corner once more and now was coming toward the river bottom. But he was still a long way off.

Dave's ears strained toward the source of the sound he had heard a moment before. He felt prickles run along his spine and down his arms. He thought angrily, "Stop it, doggone you, Dave. You're making things up in your mind. Those Indians aren't going to do anything to you."

He edged around so that the big workhorse was between him and the Indian lodges. He watched Shad Price's slow progress anxiously.

He could leave the lunch bucket, he thought. He could just hang it on the fence where Shad couldn't help seeing it. But if he did that, he'd have to explain to Shad and to himself why he'd run away.

Dave clenched his jaws angrily. He wasn't going to run away. The Indians couldn't scare him enough to make him run. Besides, Shad was almost here. He had turned the corner again and was driving his powerful team straight toward Dave.

Dave climbed over the fence and stepped out into the field as Price approached. Price called, "Whoa!" and the horses stopped. He removed the lines from around his neck and, pulling his red bandanna from his pocket, mopped his face.

He was a young man, big, red of face, blue of eye. His hair was the color of dry grass and it curled around his ears and on his neck. He glanced at the Indian lodges, then grinned at Dave.

"Brought my lunch pail, did you?" Price said. "You saved me a trip back to the agency. I've made one trip back there already and I'll never get this plowing done if I keep traipsing back and forth."

"Why did you have to go back?" Dave asked. "Break something on the plow?"

Price shook his head. He glanced at the Indian lodges again and said, "A couple of young Indians with rifles told me I'd better stop. Johnson's boy Tim and another kid. I just went to Mr. Meeker's office to be sure he realized what he might be stirring up."

"What'd he say?" Dave asked.

Shad Price smiled. "Now what do *you* think he said, Dave? Knowin' him, what would you say he told me to do?"

"Keep plowing," Dave replied.

He tried to imitate the clipped way Meeker had of speaking, and then felt ashamed of himself for mocking the man. Meeker was stubborn and he might very well be wrong about the Utes, but he was honest and he was acting according to his convictions.

Price nodded. "Right. That's exactly what he said, so I came back and started plowing again."

"Seen anything more of the Utes who told you to stop?"

Price shook his head. "No, but I guess that don't mean I won't." He glanced toward the lodges uneasily. "You know, it gives a man the shivers, plowing along next to the high sagebrush yonder. Every time I turn my back on it, I feel a spot right between my shoulder blades begin to ache."

"You said one of the boys was Johnson's son Tim," Dave said. "The other one wasn't Tono, was it?"

Tono was Dave's Indian friend, a boy his own age who had lived for a while with a white family in Utah after his father died. Later he had been taken by an uncle who had brought him to the White River Reservation. Tono spoke English almost as well as Dave.

Price shook his head. "Nope. I know Tono. It wasn't him."

Dave sighed with relief. Price reached for the lunch pail and Dave handed it to him. He stooped over and

5

stuck it under a clump of tall grass next to a fence post, where it would be shaded from the sun. He walked back to the plow, picked up the lines, and put them around his neck. He placed his big hands on the handles of the plow, shouting, "Hah! Giddap!"

The horses began to move and the plow bit into the sod. The lurch threw Price slightly to one side before he regained control of the plow. He turned his head and grinned amiably at Dave. In that instant Dave heard the shot.

At first he thought it was a harness strap snapping, but almost immediately realized it was not. He opened his mouth to yell at Price, but before he could make a sound, he heard a second shot. It was followed by a loud *clang* as the bullet struck the plow and ricocheted away into space, whining like a bee.

Price didn't stand there wondering what had happened. He knew. He freed himself from the lines and dived for the high grass ten feet away at the edge of the plowed ground. A third shot rang out.

Price wriggled through the grass toward Dave, who had raised his head enough to peer toward the Ute lodges. The movement must have been seen by the hidden riflemen because the rifle cracked again. This time Dave saw black powder smoke billow up from a high clump of sagebrush and glimpsed something dark behind the clump.

Price reached the fence where Dave was crouched. He whispered, "Keep down, Dave! For gosh sakes, keep down."

Dave started to speak, but his voice came out a croak. He cleared his throat and asked hoarsely, "What are we going to do?"

He was suddenly glad that Price was here with him. He repeated, "What are we going to do?"

"I know one thing I'm going to do," Price said grimly. "I'm going to stop plowing."

"You can't just leave the horses there," Dave said.

Price glanced at him. "If I try to unhitch them from that plow, I'll get myself killed."

"Maybe they'll hear the shots at the agency."

Price grimaced. "What can they do even if they hear them? Come boilin' down here and take on the whole Ute tribe?"

Dave shook his head. He could not imagine Nathan Meeker with a rifle in his hand. Neither could he imagine Meeker giving the others orders to arm themselves and begin shooting Indians. That was not Meeker's way. But he might come out here by himself, walking slowly and deliberately as if he could turn the bullets aside with words.

Price shifted position to make himself more comfortable. Dave said, "You act like this was some kind of a game. What if they're sneaking up on us right now?"

"What if they are, young Dave? What do you think we ought to do about it?"

"I think we ought to get out of here," said Dave.

"And leave the horses hitched to that plow? I thought you said we couldn't leave the horses here."

"You're making fun of me," Dave said.

7

"No, I'm not. No, sir. I'm as scared as you, every bit. Only I don't see what we can do right now but wait. If those Indians are fixin' to kill us and take our hair, nothin' we can do will change anything. We can't fight rifles with bare hands."

He paused and said at last, "On the other hand, if all they want is to scare me away from that plow, then they've done what they set out to do."

"We could crawl back to the house. Or out of rifle range, at least."

Price shook his head. "No. No Indian is going to make me crawl no matter how scared I am."

Dave wished he hadn't suggested that they crawl away. Now he felt as though he had to make up for it. He said rashly, "Maybe I could unhitch the team. They won't figure I'm going to plow."

"Huh-uh. You stay right where you are. Meeker would have a fit if anything happened to you, being a friend of your folks and all. You . . ."

His voice trailed off. Dave was already up and walking deliberately toward the plow as though no Indians were within one hundred miles. His hands were shaking so violently that he could hardly unhitch the team, but he managed it. He snapped the tugs up out of the way and picked up the lines.

His voice was hoarse as he yelled, "Hah! Giddap!"

The horses moved ahead, turning immediately in response to Dave's hands on the lines. They headed back toward the agency.

Dave's back ached between the shoulder blades the way Price said his had, but he didn't look around. He heard the workhorse he had ridden out to the pasture coming along behind on the other side of the fence.

"Good work," Shad Price said almost beneath his breath when he caught up with Dave. "Good work, young Dave. You sure got us out of that."

Dave was still scared and he knew they weren't out of danger yet, but he felt an exhilaration that was new to him. His face was hot and flushed with embarrassment at Price's unexpected praise.

In the distance, Dave saw several men clustered in front of Meeker's house, their faces white as they stared in the direction from which the shots had come.

He turned his head and grinned tightly at Price. And Price grinned back. "By golly, Dave, we forgot my lunch."

"Let's not go back for it now," Dave said.

Both of them laughed hilariously, but with a nervous shrillness neither one could conceal.

CHAPTER
TWO

For once Meeker did not have much to say to either Dave or Shadrach Price. He walked to the corral and watched them in silence as they unharnessed the horses and turned them into the enclosure.

"Neither of you are hurt, are you?" the agent asked.

Dave and Price shook their heads. Price grinned, and said, "Only our feelings, Mr. Meeker. And I reckon the plow's got a bullet gouge in it."

Dave thought Meeker's face turned pale. The agent said, "That close, eh?" and frowned, his shoulders slumping. He was silent for a moment, his gaze on the Ute lodges, and then he said, "Find something else to do for the present, Price. Dave can help you if he wants."

"Yes, sir."

Dave and Price watched Meeker walk back to the house, his shoulders still slumped. His steps lacked the spring Dave remembered, and his head was not thrust forward and held high the way it had been when Dave first saw him on one of his visits to Greeley weeks ago.

Dave glanced at Price. "What are we going to do?"

10

"Something easier on our nerves than plowing while rifle bullets buzz around our heads. Come on. There's harness that needs fixin' in the barn."

Dave followed Price to the big log barn. Price got the harness out and, sitting on a couple of chunks of firewood that had not been split, they started to repair sections that were worn or ripped. The warm September sun streamed in through the open door.

They had been working for about half an hour when Dave heard the door slam at the rear of the barn. A moment later he saw Tono walking toward him.

Tono was not as tall as Dave, lacking two inches of his height, but he was broader of shoulder. His legs were short and slightly bowed.

He was dressed in deerskin pants, dark and shiny with grease and smoke. He wore a white man's shirt that was bright red, and white man's cowboy boots. His hair was long, lying in two braids, one on each side of his head.

Sitting squarely atop his head was a white man's black derby hat. Tono was very proud of his hat. Dave had never seen him when he wasn't wearing it. It was decorated with a single turkey feather, which was stuck in the band and swept from front to rear.

Tono's face was broad and dark, with high cheekbones and a wide, good-natured mouth. His eyes were like black coals above a nose that was flat and very broad. Right now his eyes were grave.

"I heard the shots," Tono said, "but I did not know they were shooting at you. I am sorry, Dave."

11

Dave could grin about the incident now, and did. "No harm done. Neither of us got hit."

"We might have been, though," Price said.

"No." Tono shook his head. "If they had wanted to hit you, they would. They are both good shots."

Price snorted. "Don't try to tell me that. One of their bullets hit the plow. You can't make me believe they can aim that close and know they're going to miss."

Tono glanced at him and frowned. "I did not know they hit the plow."

"Well, you know it now." Neither Price's tone nor his eyes were friendly.

Tono fidgeted. "I've got to go," he said to Dave. "I wanted you to come to the horse races this afternoon. I am going to race my spotted horse against that of Sanchez and I want you to see me win."

"But your racetrack got plowed up," Dave said.

Tono nodded. "Now we have to race on the road."

"All right, I'll come," Dave said. "I sure hope you win."

Tono smiled. "I will win. You will see." He turned and walked silently back to the rear of the barn. A moment later Dave heard the door slam.

"You're not going, are you?" Price asked.

"Tono's my friend," Dave said. "He didn't have anything to do with the shots that were fired at us."

"He's a red Indian all the same," Price said doggedly. "They're all alike."

Dave frowned. He didn't want to argue with Price, but he couldn't accept a sweeping statement like that, either. He asked, "Are all white men alike?"

12

"The Indians say they are," Price said.

He was grinning faintly, admitting by his grin that Dave's point was well taken.

Both returned to their work and conversation lagged. When the dinner bell sounded at noon, they put the harness away and headed for the well to wash.

Meeker was preoccupied when Dave asked him if he could have the afternoon off to go to the horse race. He seemed to have trouble concentrating enough to make a decision. Finally he said, "You know I do not approve of horse racing and gambling."

"Yes, sir," Dave said, "but, you see, Tono and I don't gamble on the races. We just like to see the horses run."

Meeker seemed about to refuse and Dave braced himself for it, but suddenly the agent's expression changed. He said, "All right, Dave. Keep your ears open and pay attention to how the Utes act toward you. I have an important decision to make and I need all the information I can get."

Dave nodded, even though he did not entirely understand what Meeker meant by the things he had just said. He left Meeker's office hurriedly and strode up the road toward the cottonwood.

The Indians were already assembling. He saw Johnson, the big medicine man who was the father of one of the boys who had done the shooting that morning. Douglas, the chief, was there. He was a short, chunky man with a thin moustache. He wore a cut-off blue jacket that had once been a U. S. Army blouse. A great variety of brass buttons decorated it.

Jack was another important leader, a tall, slender man who was built more like an Arapaho than a Ute. He was much younger than Douglas and more aggressive and actually had a greater following among the White River warriors than Douglas did. He was dressed in buckskin, with a filled cartridge belt buckled around his waist.

Colorow was there, too, the most notorious beggar among the Ute chiefs. White settlers along the edge of the reservation had fed him and his band many times rather than have trouble with them. He was a grossly fat man who never seemed to get enough to eat. Dave had heard Colorow was born a Comanche. In any case, he was a Ute chief now with a small following.

Dave searched the crowd for Tono's face. He saw him at last, standing beside a brown and white spotted pony. Other horses and riders were ranged along the starting line.

He pushed toward Tono, thinking that here in this crowd were the two young Utes who had shot at him and Price this morning. He discovered that he was not afraid of mingling with these Indians. He knew he was safe.

The two had not fired those shots because they hated him, or even disliked him. They had no reason to, except perhaps for the fact that his skin was white.

Tono saw him and waved. When Dave reached him, he was grinning. "I am to race Sanchez over there — the one standing beside that dun-colored horse."

Dave nodded. He was watching the start of another race in which five horses were participating. They

14

pounded away, abreast on the narrow road, cheered on by the high, yipping yells of the Ute spectators.

Most of the Indians were busily making bets with each other on the outcome of the race. The stakes ranged from blankets to money, tobacco, cartridges, and even horses.

Dave's gaze swept the crowd. No longer were they the sullen, angry Indians he had seen visiting Meeker's office. They were like happy, carefree children now.

Dave grinned. Children, my eye, he told himself as he looked at the scars on some of the men, at the weapons most of them carried. Still, the similarity persisted in his mind in spite of the contradiction his eyes saw.

Now Tono and Sanchez were mounted, holding their prancing horses in, waiting for the gun that would signal them to start. The muscles in Tono's arms strained. His eyes gleamed. His mouth was tight with excitement. His gaze searched for Dave and found him. He gave a bare half-inch nod and grinned.

The Utes surrounding the two were yelling now, yelling encouragement at one or the other, depending on how they had bet on the race. The gunshot sounded, and the two pounded away recklessly, disappearing almost immediately in a cloud of dust.

Preparations were already under way for the start of another race. Dave pushed free of the crowd and walked to the upper side of the road. From there he could see that Tono had won, and Dave knew how proud he would be, how much the victory meant to him.

Dave climbed the hill and found a gray shale rock to sit on. All around him the Indian children played and scuffled, or just sat and solemnly watched the excitement below.

They paid little attention to Dave. It was almost as though for this short time he was one of them.

Puzzled, he stared back in the direction of the agency. He could see the narrow strip of brown plowed earth bordering the green of the horse pasture.

Meeker might be right, he thought, when he said the Indians had to farm and raise cattle instead of horses, and live in houses the way the whites did, if they expected to survive in the years to come.

The trouble was that the agent was going about it all wrong. Even Dave, as young as he was, could see that. Meeker was forcing things too fast. The Utes would not be changed overnight from hunters, horse racers, warriors, into staid and peaceful men following a plow.

Dave knew that if Meeker kept trying to force them to change their ways, they'd rebel and fight. Then he and Price and the others at the agency would be right in the middle, and Tono would become his enemy.

CHAPTER
THREE

After the shooting incident, an uneasy calm settled over the White River valley, over the hide tepees of the Utes, over the buildings at the agency. Along the crystal-clear White River, cottonwoods and willows flamed, and beneath the tall cottonwoods shorter serviceberry brush was beginning to turn brown and red.

Yet there was still green among the yellow leaves on the trees, even though the nights were chilly with the promise of winter, now not far away. Up on the slopes the deer had turned steel gray, and the last of the drying velvet had disappeared from the horns of the big bucks.

And out in the horse pasture of the Utes, Shadrach Price's plow sat askew, its plowshare still in the ground, rusting, because nobody would go out and pull it back to the agency.

About a week after the shooting, following the noon meal, Dave hitched a team to one of the wagons and headed up the hill north of the river to continue hauling in the winter's supply of wood, a job he had begun some time before.

The wood had already been cut by Shad Price and a couple of other men. The cedars had been left where they were felled and trimmed. Dave walked along on the ground beside the team, leading them by the halter of the near horse.

Upon reaching a cedar log, he would stop the horses, go around behind, and drag the log up on the load. It was heavy work, but Dave liked it, thinking of the muscles he would have when he returned to Greeley in the spring.

He finished loading in midafternoon. Stepping up into the seat, he unwound the lines from the brake handle. But for a moment he remained motionless, looking down at the valley, at the agency buildings, at the Ute lodges strung out along the river for more than a mile. He frowned as he stared at the peaceful scene. The feeling of trouble was still in the air, in spite of the fact that nothing had happened since the plowing incident.

In the distance, Dave saw Frank Dresser, who had come from Greeley at the same time he had, working with another of the Greeley boys down below. They were sawing up the cedar logs with a two-man saw. The two spent almost as much time looking around for Indians as they did working.

They were all scared, Dave thought, and they admitted it. It was no disgrace. Anybody would be scared if he met a grizzly bear up here in the cedars while cutting or hauling wood. And when you heard the Ute drums beating every night, thump-dum-dum, thump-dum-dum, it sent prickles up and down your spine and kept you from going to sleep. It was like meeting a grizzly bear.

18

The rumor of trouble had reached even Greeley, out on the plains east of the Rockies, and some of the boys had received letters from their folks telling them to come home. But they all agreed that running from their fear would be a disgrace.

Dave wrote once a week to his folks. Some of the other boys wrote more often. Frank Dresser admitted with a little grin that he wrote every day, even with the mail as irregular as it was. Dave guessed Frank was just plain homesick and had to admit he had the same malady, though perhaps not as bad as Frank.

Dave jolted down the rutted, two-track trail, occasionally using the brake to hold the wagon back. It was funny, he thought, the way things worked out. He remembered how much he had wanted to escape from the little town of Greeley. It was a new town, having been started only nine years before. Maybe the time would come when it would be a good town, where Dave would want to live, but right now he guessed it was about the worst place to live in the whole state of Colorado.

He'd been sick and tired of going to school, of doing chores, of hunting for jobs and not finding anything. So when Meeker had come to Greeley seeking help for the agency, Dave had jumped at the chance. Anything to get out of Greeley, he had told himself. Anything. Of course, there had been the promise of adventure, too.

Eight years ago, when he had come to Colorado with his parents, he had expected to see Indians and buffalo and cowboys. But all he'd seen were a couple of run-down cowboys. There were certainly no Buffalo and few Indians left around Greeley anymore. Just sagebrush and cactus and dust, things that don't go into a boy's dreams of adventure and excitement in the West.

Well, he hadn't seen any buffalo at the agency, but he'd seen Indians — hundreds of them. And quarrelsome ones to boot. Indians who scowled and yelled at Meeker. Indians who shot at a man when he was trying to plow.

As Dave approached the L-shaped building that was Meeker's house and office, he saw Johnson, the Ute medicine man, cross the road in front of the house and go inside. Dave drove up behind the house to the pile of cedars he'd hauled in previously. He wrapped the lines around the brake handle and stepped down.

He couldn't help thinking about Johnson as he rolled a cedar log from the top of the wagon onto the pile on the ground. Even though his son had shot at Dave and Shad Price, the medicine man was Meeker's friend. He was probably the only Indian on the whole reservation who had been convinced by the agent's argument that the white man's way of life was superior to the Indian's.

All the others had resisted the idea stubbornly. Tono had told him only yesterday that most of them were prepared to resist the idea with force if Meeker kept pushing so hard. Tono said that trouble was on the way because Meeker wasn't going to change. It would come in "maybe one sleep, maybe ten," he had said, mocking the way some of the Indians talked.

Johnson was a fine-looking Indian, but Dave had caught a glimpse of his face as he crossed the road to the house and he wasn't his usual, pleasant self. His face had been ugly with anger. Maybe he was finally going to make trouble for Meeker.

Suddenly Dave wished that he had his rifle. The silence at the house was ominous. He wondered if there were other Indians skulking around. Perhaps Johnson had brought help with him.

Dave's rifle was in the bunkhouse and he had a notion to go after it, but changed his mind. There were several other white men in sight, older men who would have gone after their guns if it had appeared necessary. Frank Dresser was just outside the milk house. Fred Shepard and George Eaton were yonder in front of the stable. He'd better leave this to them, Dave thought.

He had almost finished unloading when he heard Mrs. Meeker scream. He dropped the log in his hands and ran around the house. Shepard and Eaton were a step ahead of him. Just as Dave cleared the corner and reached the front of the house, he saw Johnson slam the agent against the hitching rail.

A moment later, Shepard and Eaton grabbed the medicine man and held him. Dave rushed past them to Meeker, who was slumped against the hitching rail.

"Are you hurt?" Dave asked breathlessly.

Meeker didn't answer until he saw that Johnson had been released and was stalking away toward his lodge. Then he said wearily, "I don't think so. Just shaken up."

Dave took an arm. "I'll help you inside."

Fred Shepard took the agent's other arm and together they helped Meeker into his office. He dropped into the chair at his desk. Mrs. Meeker fluttered around, asking if he was all right. Ignoring his wife for the moment, Meeker picked up a pillow and arranged it on the left arm of his chair. This done, he laid his arm on it gingerly.

Several weeks before, he had injured the arm returning to the agency from Rawlins. The wagon in which he had been riding had overturned on a grade coming down to the Williams Fork and he had been pinned underneath. His arm had hurt him ever since. Its slow healing had, of course, added to his worries.

He raised his head and shook it, his gaze on his wife. "I'm all right, Arvilla. You can go back to whatever you were doing."

She hesitated, her eyes searching his face anxiously. Then she left the room, apparently satisfied that he was all right. He looked up and smiled wryly at the men. His right hand gingerly explored his ribs and chest.

"Nothing broken." He paused a moment and then said wonderingly, "I was sitting right here in this chair when Johnson took me by the shoulders and lifted me and rushed me outside. The next thing I knew he threw me against the hitching rail. I guess he knocked the wind out of me."

He took a long breath, his gaze fixed on the wall above Dave's head. More to himself than to the men in front of him, he said, "What really hurts is that I considered Johnson my good friend. I thought he was the one Indian here who understood what I have tried to do for him and for the other Utes. Now, to have him turn against me this way . . ." He smiled wanly.

The men continued to stand around Meeker, wondering what the trouble had been about. When it became evident that the agent was not going to tell them anything without prodding, Dave said, "I saw him cross the road and come toward the house. He sure looked mad about something."

"He was furious," Meeker said. "It seems to be the old problem of my ordering the land plowed. I should think it would be obvious even to Johnson that we can't get a crop of wheat next summer if we don't plow the land this fall. Then, of course, he accused me again of sending lies to Washington."

Dave glanced at Eaton and Shepard and looked quickly away. Their expressions were a mixture of sympathy for Meeker and disapproval of his stubbornness. Everyone except Meeker seemed to understand how the Utes felt about having their horse pastures plowed, but Meeker seemed obsessed on the subject of raising wheat. He had even ordered a threshing machine, a gristmill, and two more breaking plows. They had not arrived at the agency yet, but when they did, they would add to the Indians' anger.

"None of them like the idea of having the land plowed," Dave said, surprised at his rashness. "They're afraid they won't have enough winter pasture for their pony herd."

Meeker snorted in disgust. "What if they don't? Why should they keep all those ponies anyway? I told Johnson he'd be better off if he shot his ponies. That's what set him off, I guess."

For a moment, no one said anything. Dave was thinking that the agent should have known better than to say a thing like that to Johnson. He might just as well have told the medicine man to kill his family or some of his Ute friends. Either act would seem like murder to a Ute.

"If you're sure you're all right," Eaton said, "we'll go back to work."

"Yes. I'm quite all right," Meeker said tonelessly.

Eaton and Shepard left the office. Dave hesitated, not sure he should leave. Meeker was sixty-two years old, but right now he looked much older and very frail. Dave felt sorry for him, but he knew there was nothing he could do. He turned reluctantly and left the house.

When he caught up with the others, Eaton was saying, "If he doesn't know any better than to tell Johnson to shoot his ponies, we're in trouble, boys."

Shepard nodded glumly. "We'll hear drums again tonight. And one of these nights those drums will stir 'em up enough to make 'em come lookin' for white scalps."

Dave returned to the wagon in an uneasy state of mind. He finished unloading the wood and then, glancing at the sun, decided it was too late to go after another load today.

He drove to the stable, unhooked the wagon, and unhitched and watered the team. Then he turned them out to pasture. He had not written his folks for several days. He didn't know when the mail would go out, but he supposed he'd better write to them tonight. He wasn't going to tell them about all the trouble, though. It would only make them worry more.

CHAPTER
FOUR

Dave was preoccupied as he headed for the well to wash up that night. It was hard for him to understand what had happened on the reservation to completely change the feeling between Nathan Meeker and the Utes in so short a time. He remembered listening to a conversation between Meeker and his father a year ago last April, just before Meeker left Greeley to assume his duties as agent to the Utes. He had talked about "my Utes"; he had looked forward with intense satisfaction to leading them from barbarism into a "civilized" way of life.

Dave had asked Tono about the increasing hostility. His friend had said that in the beginning the Utes had been very friendly to Meeker. They had almost starved to death in previous years because supplies meant for them had spoiled in warehouses in Rawlins, 185 miles to the north in Wyoming Territory, and their former agents had seemed unable to do anything about it. But Meeker had. And, as Tono said, there was nothing like a full stomach to make you feel friendly toward the man who had filled it for you.

As Dave was thinking about the situation, the others began drifting in, to wash up — Frank Dresser, George

Eaton, Fred Shepard, and the rest. The last to come was Shad Price.

Shepard grinned at Price. "Been shot at lately, Shad?"

Price scowled, but there was humor in his eyes. He said, "It wouldn't hurt some of you jaspers to do a little worrying' about what's going on."

Shepard sobered. "After what happened to Meeker this afternoon, maybe we all ought to do a little worrying," he said.

Price looked at him questioningly. Shepard began to tell the story and the others listened, all of them grimly silent. Meeker's daughter, Josie, hammered on the gong to let them know supper was ready. They walked into the dining room and found places in silence at the long table. Flora Ellen Price, who worked in the boardinghouse for Josie Meeker, brought heaping platters of venison steak to the table and then poured coffee for the men.

Dave stared at Josie and Flora Ellen uneasily. Flora Ellen was hardly more than a girl. Even so, she had two small children, a girl named May and a boy, Johnnie. Dave was more worried about the safety of the three women here and about Flora Ellen's two children than he was about his own or that of the other men. The men had rifles and, given any chance at all, could defend themselves. The women could not.

Dave remained at the table after the meal was finished and the rest of the men had left the dining room. Josie helped Flora Ellen pick up the dishes and pile them on the worktable near the stove.

27

Besides taking the contract to feed the agency employees, Josie was also the teacher of the Ute children, but Dave knew that her teaching experiences here had been very disappointing. She'd never had more than three or four children in her school at any one time. Now she had only one, the son of Douglas, the chief.

When the table had been cleared, Josie poured a cup of coffee and sat down across from Dave. She looked tired. He was sure she had heard about her father's trouble with Johnson.

Josie smiled at him. "I never saw a boy who got enough to eat. If you're waiting for another piece of pie, I'll get it for you."

"No," Dave said. "I just wanted to talk before I went to the bunkhouse. I've got to write my folks tonight before I go to bed."

"I don't know when the mail will go out," Josie said. "I guess you've heard that the regular riders won't make the trip between the agency and Rawlins since we've been having so much trouble here."

"Did you hear about Johnson and your pa?" Dave asked.

She nodded. "I was over to the house a minute before supper. I guess nothing could have hurt him worse than having Johnson turn on him."

Dave hesitated, not sure he should say what was in his mind. Even the smartest of men have blind spots, and it was evident that Meeker was blind as far as the Ute ponies were concerned. Dave couldn't criticize the agent, or even make suggestions to him, but maybe his daughter could.

"Your pa never should have told Johnson to kill off his ponies the way he did," Dave said. "Maybe you ought to tell him."

She stirred her coffee, smiling. "Dave, my father is a good man, but he's stubborn. I can't tell him anything."

"Then he's going to get us killed," Dave said.

"Yes, that could happen," Josie agreed. "He's worried about it. In fact, he's been worried for a month or more. He thinks he may have to send for troops."

"They'd never get here in time," Dave said.

Josie said, "I suppose they couldn't. But what can we do?"

Dave said, "We could start by taking the Indians the way they are instead of trying to change them into farmers overnight. If your father would just go at it a little slow . . . Tono says the Utes almost worship their ponies. They're not going to shoot them because some white man tells them to. And they're not going to let them starve because some white man plowed up their winter pasture to sow in wheat."

Josie picked up her coffee and sipped it thoughtfully, her eyes fixed on Dave over the rim of the cup. She set it on the table, then said, "You're a smart boy, Dave. Or maybe it's your friend Tono, who's smarter than the rest of us."

"I guess it's Tono," Dave said self-consciously. "He's lived like a white man and now he's living like an Indian. He's tried both ways and he says the Indian way is best."

"There's one thing you have to understand about my father," Josie said. "It's not just that he's stubborn. He's also impatient. When he came here he had some fine plans for the Indians. But he said he couldn't wait ten or fifteen years for them to change."

Dave growled, "He won't see them change if he's dead."

"No, of course he won't," Josie agreed, frowning worriedly. "But he doesn't think they'll go that far. Or if it looks as though they will, he thinks he can get the troops here in time." She was silent for a long time after that, and at last she said reluctantly, "He loved the Utes at first, but now I think he hates them because they've defeated him."

Dave sat back on the bench and leaned against the wall, his fingers laced behind his head. Meeker probably couldn't change, any more than the Utes could change. Still, it seemed unbelievable that a man as smart as Meeker could be so stubborn and blind. It seemed ridiculous that he would endanger the lives of every white person here for a goal that was impossible.

"What are some of the plans he had for the Indians?" Dave asked.

Josie sighed. "They sound like wild dreams now, but they seemed within reach when he came. He was going to set up a model farm. He planned to buy good stallions to breed up their ponies into workhorses. He would have built a sawmill and turned some of the Ute men into lumberjacks. He planned an orchard so they could ship fruit to market. Of course, he'd have had a railroad built down here from Rawlins. They'd raise sheep and cattle and . . ."

Josie stopped and bowed her head, her lips compressed. These were, indeed, big dreams, Dave thought, compared to the reality of the last eighteen months.

"It was just a rainbow in the sky," Josie said, her head still bowed.

She rose and looked down at Dave, her face troubled. "What really hurts is to see him change from a man who loved the Utes into a man who's afraid of them and hates them and needs soldiers to protect him."

She started to turn away and then stopped. "You should have seen the way they welcomed him when he first came. They galloped around on their ponies and cheered and the children sang and laughed. It was such a good feeling to see them that way. Now when I look at them it's like seeing the sun go down in the middle of the day."

She walked across the room to help Flora Ellen finish the dishes. Dave went outside, in his mind seeing Nathan Meeker as he had been when he left Greeley for the White River Indian Agency almost a year and a half ago, tall, lean, vigorous, and younger looking than he actually was.

Now he looked older than he was. He was defeated and frightened, unable to do more than threaten to send for troops, who would put the Ute chiefs in chains and haul them off to Indian Territory to suffer and die the way the Cheyennes had.

For a moment, Dave stood outside the boardinghouse door, thinking about the letter he should write.

He was too upset, he decided, to write tonight. Maybe, if he talked to Tono, they could figure out something to do. If he and Tono could be friends, there seemed no reason why the tribe and the agency employees couldn't get along.

He turned toward the river and headed for the Ute lodges and the evening cook fires. Before long, he would hear the drums.

CHAPTER
FIVE

The road between the agency buildings and the nearest of the Indian fires was dark. The various camps, each composed of a family or groups of families, formed one continuous camp stretching along the riverbank. Dave walked swiftly, aware of blackness on both sides of the road. He hated to admit that fear could make him do anything he didn't want to do, or that it could keep him from doing something he wanted to do.

He reached the Indian fires and walked quickly among them until he came to the hide lodge where Tono lived with his uncle and his uncle's two wives. That was something else Meeker said he was going to change. A good many of the Utes had more than one wife, and such an arrangement was an outrage to Meeker's religious beliefs.

Dave supposed it *was* wrong to have more than one wife, but the Indians didn't think so and it would take some convincing on Meeker's part to make them see it the way he did.

He called and a moment later Tono stepped through the flap. By the light of the fire burning in front of the lodge, Dave saw that Tono's face was grave. His friend said, "You should not have come. What do you want?"

Dave felt an uneasiness that he'd never had with Tono before. He said, "I thought maybe we could go hunting tomorrow. Josie could use some fresh meat and I suppose you could, too."

Tono nodded, but without much enthusiasm. "All right. I'll meet you at the agency at dawn. Now you had better get back. I had better go with you. There are a lot of angry men between here and the agency, and some of them have been getting whiskey at Peck's store."

Dave started to say that he could get back all right alone, and then he stopped. Tono wasn't one to magnify danger or to get jumpy without reason. If he said it was dangerous to walk back alone, it probably was. He nodded and turned toward the agency. Tono walked beside him silently, his moccasins making only whispering sounds as his feet touched the ground.

Once there had been a closeness of understanding between them that Dave had never experienced with any white boy, but tonight it was gone. There was a strange tension in Tono. He answered Dave's questions curtly as his eyes searched the darkness on both sides of the road. He was plainly relieved when they reached the agency, and Dave was, too.

"At daylight, then," Dave said.

Tono grunted something unintelligible and stalked away. He was instantly lost in the darkness.

The drums had started to beat again. Occasionally a shrill yip would reach the agency, carried on the light evening breeze. The noise would increase as the night progressed, Dave thought, and wondered if he'd be able to sleep with that racket in his ears.

34

He went to bed immediately, not worried that he might fail to awaken in time to meet Tono at dawn. He always woke at first light, and knew he could be dressed and outside in less than five minutes. He could wash in the stream, and Tono would probably bring some dried meat for them to eat.

It was a while before he slept. The drums beat dully in his ears. The thick log walls kept out the yells of the dancers, but nothing could keep out the steady, irritating thumping of the drums.

Eventually he did sleep, and when he woke the sound of the drums was gone. The square of his window was a deep gray. Dave threw the covers back, got out of bed, and pulled on his pants and boots. He shrugged into his shirt and took his heavy short coat from the nail beside the door. He put it on, snatched his hat off another nail, and picked up his rifle from where it leaned against the wall. Then he dumped half a box of shells into the pocket of his coat. Carrying his gun, Dave went out quietly into the morning grayness.

He could see very little, just the outlines of the mountains to the east. But a moment later he saw Tono's dark shape as he stood patiently on the road.

Dave walked to his friend, remembering the way Tono had been last night, wondering if he would be that way today. He asked, "Been waiting long?"

"No."

Tono turned away immediately and headed toward the river. A horse was tied to a willow near the bank. Tono mounted and motioned for Dave to get up behind him. He removed his foot from a stirrup so that Dave could use it to mount.

Dave swung onto the horse's back. Tono kneed the animal into the river and splashed noisily across. Both boys stayed on the horse's back as he climbed out and started up the hillside through the brush and trees.

"We might just as well ride," Tono said.

Dave didn't reply. The saddle kept Tono from sliding back as the horse lunged up the slope, but it was no help to Dave. He put his arms around Tono and held on.

Tono pulled the horse to a halt at the top of the first ridge and Dave slid to the ground. He preferred to hunt on foot because he could move more quietly that way. Tono also dismounted and moved out, leading the horse. Dave hoped he wouldn't suggest that they separate. Not today. He still wanted to get Tono to talk, thinking that if he could his friend's coldness would fade.

On top of the ridge were groves of golden aspens and the thick, tangled clumps of scrub oak. Dave sat down beside one of the clumps. Tono stopped, looked at him a moment, then turned to the horse and took two chunks of dried venison from a saddlebag. He sat down beside Dave and handed one to him. His face was expressionless as he stared into the valley ahead.

Dave gnawed off a chunk of the smoky meat. It was hard to chew, but he liked the taste and knew there was a lot of nourishment in it.

The sun, which had not yet come up, had stained the eastern clouds a delicate shade of pink. Dave touched

Tono's sleeve and pointed at a buck that had just appeared below them, pleased to have seen the deer first.

Tono glanced at him and then at the buck. The animal was about three hundred yards away, standing with his head raised, looking around alertly. His coat had turned from its summer brown to a glossy, smooth gray. He was a big buck, and fat, with thick, wide-spreading horns. There were four points on one side and three on the other.

"He's coming this way," Tono whispered.

Dave didn't reply. He shifted his rifle so he could raise it instantly.

Suddenly, he felt that all of Tono's coldness of last night was gone. Once more there was the old closeness between them as they watched the big gray buck pick his way delicately up the slope. Dave looked at Tono's face. Tono met his glance and grinned. Dave grinned back. At this moment they were just two good friends sharing a great experience. The skin color that had separated them disappeared.

Dave supposed that Tono was caught, as he was, between friendship and loyalty. Tono was his friend, but he was also an Indian who owed his loyalty to his family and to his race. If the Utes went to war with the whites, he would have to stand with them.

Dave knew exactly how Tono felt because he felt that way himself. He was Tono's friend, but he was also white, and if the Utes attacked the agency, he would have to stand with the others and try to fight the

Indians off. He hoped, though, that he would never have to point a gun at Tono.

"He'll see the horse," Dave whispered.

"Uh-huh. But he won't pay any attention. He sees horses up here all the time."

Dave realized suddenly that Tono had released the horse the instant he had seen the deer. A horse wandering through the aspen trees attracted less attention than one standing still. From deer, at least.

Dave whispered, "He's not much more than two hundred yards from us now."

"He's got to be closer than that unless we want to take a chance of crippling him and following him all day," Tono said.

Dave knew that what Tono said was true. Once they had crippled a buck, and it had taken more than eight hours of trailing before they had caught up with him. Dave picked a spot about halfway between the buck and where the two of them sat. When the buck reached that spot, he would get into position to shoot.

Tono glanced at him again and grinned. "He is a nice one, Dave. You take the first shot."

Dave nodded, his eyes on the buck, and then caught something in Tono's voice that he had never noticed before. He turned his head to look at his friend. He had the sudden feeling that Tono believed this was the last time they'd be able to hunt together.

Dave wanted to tell him that it didn't have to be the last time they would hunt together. He wanted to say that the whites and Indians didn't have to fight. But it was no use. They were only boys and could do nothing about what happened between Meeker and the Utes.

The big buck picked his way up the slope gracefully. He saw the horse and paused a moment, head raised, ears pricked, body tensed to jump. Then apparently he decided it was all right. He lowered his head and came on.

He was now at the spot Dave had picked. Tono nudged his friend and Dave raised his rifle slowly, watching the deer intently as he did. He brought the rifle to his shoulder and was sighting along it when his foot dislodged a rock.

Instantly the buck's head turned toward the source of the sound. For a split second the buck stood frozen there, and in this short space of time Dave squeezed the trigger off carefully. The gun hammered against his shoulder and smoke billowed from its muzzle.

Tono's gun was also up, ready to shoot if Dave missed. But Dave hadn't missed. The buck jumped, and started to bound away, then went down, forequarters first.

Dave leaped to his feet. Tono was only a step behind him as they ran to the deer. The horse, spooked by the shot, trotted away and stopped at the crest of the ridge.

The deer was dead. Dave had fired at a spot just behind his shoulder and apparently the bullet had pierced his heart. Tono's knife was in his hand by the time he reached the fallen animal. Kneeling, he cut the deer's throat and dragged its head downhill so the animal would bleed. He glanced up at Dave and grinned his approval.

39

"Good shot, Dave," he said.

Dave felt warm from Tono's praise. Tono said, "Get hold of his hind legs. I'll open him up and clean him out."

Dave got one of the deer's hind legs in each hand. He pulled the hindquarters up the hill. Tono, working from below, opened the abdominal cavity carefully with his knife. Swiftly and expertly he removed the entrails, taking care that neither the liver nor kidneys touched the ground.

Watching intently, Dave wondered if he would ever be able to clean a deer as expertly as Tono did. Finished, Tono wiped his bloody hands on the deer's smooth hide, picked up the liver and kidneys, and placed them carefully on a rock. He and Dave pulled the deer downhill a short way and placed it on a big flat rock. Tono went after the horse, caught him, and led him into position on the downhill side of the rock.

Dave helped load the deer across the horse's back. Tono tied the deer's feet beneath the horse's belly with a rope. He cut a hole in the deer's side and poked the saddle horn through the hole so that the carcass wouldn't slip to either side. He got the liver and kidneys, tied them up in a cloth, and secured them to the saddle behind the deer.

Both boys were sweating from the exertion. The sun was well above the horizon and had driven the chill from the morning air. Tono led the horse toward the crest of the ridge and Dave walked beside the animal, steadying the carcass of the deer.

Tono led the horse down the brushy, timbered hill and across the White River to the agency. He led him into a shed and held him while Dave tied a rope to the deer's hind legs. Dave threw the rope over one of the ceiling joists and then took up slack while Tono lifted the deer clear of the horse's back. The deer hung just clear of the floor. Tono led his horse out and returned a moment later, knife in hand.

Both boys began to work rapidly, skinning the hind legs, then the back and sides, and finally the forequarters and forelegs. Tono cut the head and hide loose and dragged them to one side. The carcass was heavily layered with fat. Josie would be glad to get this meat, Dave thought. Tono sheathed his knife and turned to go. Dave said, "I thought you were going to take part of it."

"I don't need it," Tono said. "You keep all of it. You might need . . ."

He stopped, as though he had almost said something he hadn't intended to say. Dave thought that Tono had meant to say the white people at the agency would probably need the meat before long. Outnumbered by the Utes, they might be under siege for a long, long time.

Dave walked outside the shed with Tono. He suddenly wanted to keep his friend here. He had an uneasy feeling that if they separated now, they might never see each other again.

"Has anything changed, Tono?" Dave asked. "Are the Utes as angry as they were?"

Tono looked at him soberly. "More, Dave. Any little thing Meeker does might make them turn on him. Both Jack and Colorow are talking trouble. Big trouble. They say Meeker sends lies about them to Washington and that the soldiers will come because of Meeker's lies."

Dave didn't say anything, but he knew the Utes were justified in worrying. Meeker had almost reached the point of calling for soldiers. If any of the Utes made another hostile move, he would.

"Tono, no matter what happens," Dave blurted, "we can still be friends."

Tono stared at him gravely, giving no sign of agreement or disagreement. Finally he nodded, but Dave could see he did not believe that friendship was possible between them if the Utes and the whites went to war. Dave held out his hand and Tono gripped it briefly, then turned and swung to his horse's back. He thundered away down the road without looking back.

CHAPTER
SIX

Dave experienced a sudden sense of loss, as though someone who had been very close to him had died. He turned and walked briskly away to find Josie and tell her about the deer. His shoes were wet from crossing the river, but there would be plenty of time to change them later on.

He knew Josie would be in the boardinghouse, clearing the breakfast dishes from the table. He found the men lounging around in front of the building, smoking and talking. The mood of the Utes seemed to be the main topic of conversation. Dave went inside.

Josie glanced up at him. "You're late, Dave."

He nodded. "Tono and I went out and killed a deer for you. Is there anything left to eat?"

She smiled. "For a successful hunter there's always something to eat. Go on out and wash."

Dave went through the boardinghouse and out the back door. He pumped water into a basin and washed his blood-smeared hands. He dumped the water, refilled the pan, and washed his face. After drying his hands and face he went inside.

Josie had a plate waiting for him and a steaming cup of coffee to go with it. He dug in enthusiastically. There was nothing like an early morning hunt to give a fellow an appetite, he thought.

Josie's face was sober and worried as she watched him eat. At last she said softly, "My father has written out a telegram to Commissioner Hayt in Washington, asking for troops to protect him from the Utes. He hasn't sent it to Rawlins yet, but I'm afraid he will if anything else happens."

Dave glanced up. He had finished eating and had pushed his plate back. Now he pulled the coffee cup in front of him.

"What does Tono think?" Josie asked.

"He says trouble is close. Jack and Colorow are telling the Utes that your father has sent lies about them to Washington and that soldiers will be coming soon."

She left and returned a moment later with the coffeepot. She refilled his cup and poured one for herself. She sat down across from him.

"It's a pity, Dave. They can't seem to communicate with each other any more, so each is willing to believe the worst. Father says he's given up his dream of handling the Utes with love." She smiled wryly. "The big trouble with that theory was that by handling them with love, he meant making them blindly obey him."

"And now he plans to handle them by force," Dave said. "Is that it?" He realized that his words sounded as if he thoroughly disapproved of the Indian agent, and he added quickly, "I didn't aim to criticize. I know it hasn't been easy for him."

44

"No, it hasn't been easy," Josie agreed. "He doesn't want to use force with them. He knows if he does, he's lost them forever and failed in all his plans and dreams. That's why he hasn't tried to send the telegram to Rawlins. Maybe he won't send it."

Dave finished his coffee and got up. "I'd better get busy. I wasn't hired to hunt deer."

Josie smiled at him. "It's an important function just the same. If anyone says anything about your being late, you tell them to talk to me."

"Thanks," he said, grinning at her.

He wondered what would happen to Josie, her mother, and Flora Ellen Price if the Utes went on a rampage. As he stepped outside, he hesitated for a moment in front of the boardinghouse. He didn't know what he should do. He didn't want to take the team and wagon up into the cedars this morning. After what Tono had said, he felt too uneasy about that.

Dave walked to the pile of cedar logs he had unloaded from the wagon yesterday. He picked up one, about five or six inches thick, laid it on the supports, took the long one-man saw from its peg in the shed, and began to saw off a block.

He worked with a steady rhythm. The sawdust from the cut was fragrant with a tangy cedar smell. The block fell and he started another one, glad about the opportunity to do physical work. For the moment he could forget about the threatening trouble with the Utes.

The sun, now well up into the eastern sky, was warm on his back and he began to sweat. Josie left the

45

boardinghouse and crossed to the house. He heard the screen door slam as she went inside.

He could hear the comfortable rumble of Price's voice talking to someone below him as he worked on the milk house roof. A hen cackled noisily to announce a freshly laid egg. The breeze carried the smell of pine from nearby trees warmed by the morning sun.

The sounds were peaceful, and Dave associated the odors with peaceful, busy days. A fly droned around his head and he slapped at it. A pig squealed down in the pens. Dave began thinking again of his parents and of Greeley, and smiled faintly. He used to consider Greeley dull, but right now he'd settle for some dull place like Greeley, where a person wasn't wondering every second whether a bullet was going to come whistling out of nowhere and slam into him.

Dave caught himself wishing Meeker would *send* that telegram. He would feel a whole lot more secure if he knew troops were on the way.

On the other hand, he had to admit that if the soldiers did start for the agency and if the Utes found out about it, they would probably attack and burn the place to the ground. Then they could pull out of the White River valley and retreat south to Grand River (as the upper Colorado was then called), where the troops wouldn't dare follow them.

Dave worked steadily throughout the morning, stopping only long enough to drink a glass of lemonade Josie brought him at ten o'clock. At noon, he washed at the pump and went into the boardinghouse with the others.

The meal was subdued, with none of the usual bantering talk between the men that Dave had learned to expect at mealtime. Afterward Shad Price stopped Dave as he was going outside and said, "If you're tired of sawing wood, you can work on the milk house roof with me this afternoon."

Dave nodded. He liked Shad and it would be good to have somebody to talk to this afternoon. Shad pulled out his pipe and packed it. Lighting up, he blew a cloud of blue smoke into the hot fall air. A pipe has a pleasant, reassuring smell, Dave thought. Suddenly his fears seemed foolish.

He helped Price spread a thick layer of dirt over the milk house roof to insulate it from both heat and cold. When the spring rains came, weeds would sprout from the roof. Grass, too, and the roots would tie the dirt into a mat of sod that wouldn't wash away.

They finished spreading the wagon load and went after another one. By quitting time they had thrown half of the second load up onto the roof and spread it. Dave unhitched the team and led the horses away to the corral. After unharnessing them he hung the gear carefully on pegs inside the barn. He watered the horses and threw some grass hay to them. Then he headed for the pump to wash again.

He'd have to write to his folks tonight, he thought. He couldn't put it off any longer because the mail contractor, John Steele, would be arriving tomorrow afternoon. He ought to have his letter ready to go by then. If mail came for the families of other agency employees in Greeley and his folks didn't get anything from him, they'd think he was sick.

He ate supper in silence. Afterward, as the sun dipped toward the pine-clad mountains to the west, he went to his room, got paper and pencil, and began to write.

In the quiet of his room, conflict with the Utes seemed more impossible than ever. It would continue to seem that way until the shrill cries of the dancing Indians drifted through the open window, until the drums began to beat.

He finished the letter quickly, put it into an envelope, addressed and sealed it. He carried the letter to Meeker's house, where he dropped it into a box marked "Outgoing Mail."

As he returned to his room, he realized he had never changed his wet shoes. They were dry by now, he supposed, and it was probably better that he had worn them all day. They would have gotten stiff if he'd taken them off to dry.

He walked slowly through the fading evening light. The Ute drums had started again, the sound oppressive to his ears. Suddenly he wanted to run, wanted to get away from here before it was too late.

But there was no place he could run. The White River Indian Agency was squarely in the middle of the Ute reservation, and there were Indians on all sides, like a menacing, hostile wall.

CHAPTER
SEVEN

On Wednesday, in the late afternoon, John Steele arrived from Rawlins. He was the first white man to have made the long trip from Rawlins to the agency in quite a while. After supper Dave, Shad Price, and some of the others drifted toward the porch of Meeker's house, where Steele sat talking to the Indian agent.

Meeker did not send them away. He seemed, instead, to welcome their nearness. Dave sat on the steps in the twilight listening to the throbbing drums.

Steele said angrily, "Listen to those blasted savages. They're up to something. I'm not the only one who thinks so, either, believe me. I can't get riders to carry the mail, so I have to carry it myself. I'm beginning to wish I'd never heard of the mail contract between Rawlins and the agency.

"Joe Rankin won't touch it with a ten-foot pole. Says it's worth a man's life to ride through the reservation now. Charlie Lowry says the same thing and so does Mike Sweet. Black Wilson will make the ride, but I've got to pay him double, and he won't come if he doesn't feel like it.

"I tell you, there's something wrong with a government that won't protect its taxpayers. I took this

49

mail contract in good faith, and now these redskins are about to put me out of business."

Meeker said doubtfully, "I have composed a telegram to Commissioner Hayt asking for protection."

Steele brightened immediately. "Why didn't you say so, Mr. Meeker? I'll take it with me in the morning and put it on the wire at Rawlins the minute I get to town. In four days the War Department in Washington will have your request. In a couple of weeks it ought to be safe for a man to carry the mail down here again."

"Well, I don't know . . ."

"What do you mean, you don't know? They're going to murder you and your whole outfit, Mr. Meeker, if you don't get troops in here."

Meeker shook his head sadly. "If I call for troops it will be the end of everything I planned for the Utes. And besides, I'm afraid soldiers coming may only set them off."

"It don't pay to be afraid of them red-skinned devils, Mr. Meeker," Steele said compellingly. "You'd ought to do what needs to be done and not worry about how the savages are going to take it."

"I suppose you're right."

Dave couldn't keep silent anymore. His voice was shaking from his boldness in speaking up, but he went on anyway. "He's wrong, Mr. Meeker. You're the one who's right. I've been in their village and I've talked to Tono and I know that troops coming in *will* set them off. Maybe I shouldn't say this, Mr. Meeker, but you've pushed them too far the way it is. You plowed their racetrack and started on their horse pastures, and if you

50

do one more thing, like bringing in the troops, they're going to fight."

Steele stared at him, his eyes cold. "Who's this kid to be talking to you like this? Is he the agent or are you?"

Meeker frowned. He said, "That will be enough, Dave."

"Yes, sir. I'm sorry. But it's true. They're all ready to explode. Maybe Mr. Steele doesn't know it because he just got here, but I've listened to their talk and I've seen the way they look at me. And I know they might have killed Mr. Price if he hadn't stopped plowing when he did."

"Dave!" Meeker said angrily.

Dave subsided, wondering suddenly if his arguments had not succeeded in doing exactly what he had wished to avoid. Meeker might now send the telegram if only to prove he wasn't going to be told what to do by any seventeen-year-old employee.

Maybe he was only seventeen, but he had a right to speak, for if trouble came he was in it with the rest of them. Still, the responsibility for the safety of all the whites at the agency rested squarely upon Meeker's shoulders, and he would have to decide what should be done.

If Steele had not come to the agency today, it was possible Meeker would never have sent the telegram, Dave thought. But Steele had come and he was urging Meeker to send it immediately. Meeker, at his wits' end, disillusioned and frightened, wanted someone to tell him what to do. He would probably send the telegram north with Steele.

Dave was suddenly more scared than he had ever been before. The Indians might attack the agency tonight. No one could predict what they might do.

Dave got up and walked away. The fires in the Ute villages were spots of orange in the night, casting weird, flickering shadows on the trees. The drums thumped on.

The mid-September days were hot and still. In spite of the tension or maybe because of it, they dragged for Dave. They dragged for the others at the agency, too, but everyone went about his work, determined not to show the Utes any fear. Sometimes a group of Ute braves would ride their horses toward the agency, yelling shrilly and brandishing their weapons, only to stop and stare sullenly at the whites who were moving back and forth, trying to appear unconcerned.

Ute Jack, one of the subchiefs, stalked down the road to Meeker's house one day, scowling fiercely at everyone he passed. Dave saw him climb the steps to the porch, cross it, and enter the house without knocking.

Dave moved closer to the house so that he would be near if Jack should attack Meeker the way Johnson had. He didn't know how much help he would be because he was no match physically for the powerful Ute, but at least he would try.

He heard the Ute chief's harsh voice and his pidgin English words. "Utes want hunt. Wyoming. Now. Cold weather come pretty soon. Utes need blankets go on hunt. Want blankets. Now. Want heap blankets."

Meeker's voice sounded frightened as he said, "I can't issue you blankets, Jack. It isn't time to issue them."

"What mean, time?" Jack demanded. "Utes need blankets. Blankets in storehouse. You give now."

Meeker's voice, still frightened, had the patient quality of a man speaking to a child. "You don't understand, Jack. The government has rules, and since I work for the government, I have to obey the rules."

"Who blankets belong to?"

"They belong to the Utes, Jack. They were sent here for the Utes."

"Then give Utes blankets."

Meeker said, "If I do, they'll be gone by the time cold weather comes. Your braves will take them to Peck's store and trade them for whiskey, and when it gets cold they'll expect me to give them more."

Jack's voice rose as he said, "Heap mad, Jack. Mebbe go break door. Take blankets. All Utes heap mad. Meeker plow racetrack. Make Utes race on road. Meeker plow horse pasture. Tell Utes kill horses. Meeker big fool. By and by mebbe Utes shoot big fool Meeker instead of horses."

"Are you threatening me?"

"No threaten. Tell."

Meeker's voice was trembling with rage. "You leave now if you have said what you came to say. I am not afraid of you. Perhaps what people have been telling me is right — you don't understand anyone trying to help you live a better life. All you want to do is gamble and hunt and lounge around in the sun, living worthless lives while your women and children do your work."

"No leave," Jack said stubbornly. "Want blankets."

"You will not get any blankets from me. You're not even supposed to go hunting in Wyoming. You're not supposed to leave the reservation. If you do leave, I may be forced to send for troops to bring you back."

There was a long, ominous silence after that. Dave felt the blood drain out of his face. His hands began to shake. What would Jack do now? It had been a mistake for Meeker to mention troops. He still did not fully understand the Indians' fear of the soldiers, or what that fear might make them do if they were pushed.

When Jack finally spoke, his voice was as ominous as the silence had been. "No send for soldiers. Utes not afraid of soldiers. Kill all soldiers that come." He paused, and then said slowly, "Mebbe kill Meeker, too."

Meeker did not speak again. After a moment the door slammed open and Jack stalked furiously onto the porch. He saw Dave standing at the window and scowled savagely. He strode away, every movement eloquent of the fury boiling in him.

Dave hurried away. He didn't want Meeker to see him here. He had not been eavesdropping intentionally, and he didn't want the agent to think he had.

From behind a shed he watched the powerful figure of Jack until the chief disappeared into the trees. The situation was certainly not getting any better, he thought ruefully. Everything Meeker did or said only seemed to add to the tension and make things worse.

Dave had not seen Tono since the morning they had killed the buck, and that had been more than two weeks ago. Although everyone at the agency knew Meeker had finally sent the telegram, no one knew whether troops were on the way or not. For more than a week the white people had lived in daily fear of their lives, despite the way they scoffed at the danger among themselves to keep their spirits up.

Mrs. Meeker was pale and seemed to Dave more shaky than she had been. Josie hurried from one task to another as though keeping busy were the only way she could blot out of her mind the danger they were in. Flora Ellen Price was as silent as a frightened child, which indeed she was.

Ute Jack had not been seen by any of the white people since the day of the argument over blankets. Everyone supposed he had taken his braves north for the fall hunt in Wyoming, despite Meeker's direct order to him not to go.

Early in the afternoon of September 26, Dave was disturbed by a strange feeling he was being watched. He had worked steadily at sawing blocks of cedar. Now, in spite of the feeling that someone was watching, he did not look up until a block dropped from the end of the log. Then he straightened up, laid down the saw, and casually wiped the sweat from his forehead with the back of his hand.

A moment later he heard Tono call from the tall brush along the fence about fifty feet away. Dave glanced in that direction and saw his friend standing there, practically concealed by a large clump of sagebrush. He walked quickly to where his friend stood.

Dave sensed that the Ute boy was more concerned with concealing himself from anyone who might be watching from the Indian villages than from the white people at the agency. As soon as Dave reached him, Tono whispered urgently, "Troops are coming. There will be trouble between the Utes and the men at the agency. I want you to leave — now. Otherwise I am afraid you will be killed."

"How do you know troops are on the way?" Dave asked excitedly.

"Jack took his hunters north the day before yesterday to hunt in Wyoming as they do every fall. Yesterday at Bear River they found a soldier camp. A scout brought back the word today. The soldiers are coming here. My people think they are going to murder all of us the way Custer murdered the Cheyennes on the Washita and the way Chivington did at Sand Creek."

"They won't do that," Dave said. "They're just coming to make sure the Utes don't bother Meeker and the rest of us here at the agency."

"That is why I want you to run away. My people may not wait for the soldiers to arrive. They may attack the agency before the soldiers can get this far."

Dave sucked in a long breath, his heart pounding. "They wouldn't be foolish enough for that. It would be the end of them."

Tono looked at him soberly. "I'm one of them, Dave. I know them and I have heard their talk. They can't change the way they are or the way they live. They'd

56

rather die. They're proud they were the first Indians in America to use horses. Maybe that's why they love their horses so. Maybe that's why they like to move around the way they do. They don't want to farm. And the men don't want to do women's work. They want to hunt and fight so they can feel like men."

Dave said, "Meeker says they're going to have to change. He says they'll have to learn to live like the white men or die. That's why he's tried so hard to teach them to farm and raise cattle and sheep."

Tono said, "He'd just as well try to tame a mountain lion."

Dave was silent for a time. At last he said, "I'll have to tell Mr. Meeker what you said."

"I know. I also know he will not believe you. He will not believe until they shoot at him." Tono keep glancing nervously toward the Indian camp, plainly not wanting to be seen talking to Dave.

"Thanks, Tono. Thanks for warning me," Dave said.

"But you will not leave?"

Dave shook his head. "Not unless everyone else does. I couldn't run away all by myself."

Tono shook his head. "No. I didn't think you would." He looked steadily into Dave's eyes for a moment, then turned and disappeared into the high brush along the fence, heading toward the river.

Dave walked thoughtfully back to the pile of cedar logs. He had learned some of the Utes' history after coming here to work. He knew how much they loved their independence and freedom. He had heard the stories of how they had stolen horses from the

Spaniards near Santa Fe, New Mexico, more than two hundred years ago. He knew how much they loved the mountains where they lived, even though they sometimes drifted east to hunt buffalo on the plains. They were deadly enemies of the Arapaho and Cheyenne, who called them "black Indians" because their skin was dark.

As with all humans, he supposed, pride was as necessary to the Indians as food and drink. They took pride in their heritage, strength, courage, and their hunting and riding skills. To their way of thinking, if they let Meeker put them behind a plow, digging in the earth like squaws, they would lose their pride. It was as simple as that, only Meeker couldn't understand.

Dave stood motionless for a long time, staring at the pile of cedar blocks. Then, making his decision, he strode decisively toward the agent's house.

CHAPTER
EIGHT

As Dave crossed the porch he saw that the door was standing open. He knocked and Arvilla Meeker answered. She was wearing a heavy woolen sweater, despite the warmth of the day. Even with the sweater, she shivered as if she had a chill.

Mrs. Meeker tried to smile at Dave, but it was not much of a smile. Dave said, "I'd like to see Mr. Meeker, ma'am."

"Of course, David. Come in."

He went into the house, which was cooler than outside. Meeker's deep voice said, "Come in, Dave. Come in."

Dave went into the office. Meeker sat at his desk, which was littered with papers. He was just sitting there not doing anything. He asked in a tired voice, "What did you want to see me about?"

"Tono was just here, Mr. Meeker."

"Yes?"

"He says that Ute Jack took a bunch of hunters north to hunt in Wyoming and they found a soldier camp at Bear River."

Meeker slumped with relief. He said, his voice barely audible, "Thank God the soldiers are on the way."

Dave stared at him, puzzled. Surely Meeker realized how dangerous it was for the Utes to know soldiers were on the way. He said, "Tono came to warn me, sir. He wanted me to leave the agency. He says the Indians are afraid they'll be massacred the way the Cheyennes were at Sand Creek and at the Washita. He thinks they may attack us here at the agency before the troops arrive."

"They wouldn't dare do that," Meeker said.

The words were more certain than the tone he used, Dave thought. He said, "Couldn't we all just leave, Mr. Meeker? We could come back when the trouble is over."

Meeker stared at him for an instant. Dave glanced away, ashamed, but Meeker seemed to understand. He said, "Being afraid is nothing to be ashamed of, Dave. We've all been afraid lately. I doubt that you'd go even if it was possible. You didn't run when those shots were fired at you and Mr. Price, and I don't think you really want to run away now."

Meeker paused, then said, "Besides, I don't believe anything serious is going to happen. If I did, I would insist that everyone leave immediately. The Utes may not understand me or the way I have tried to handle them, but they most certainly understand force. Did Tono say how many troops were in the camp that Jack and his hunters found?"

"No, sir. He didn't say. But I guess Ute Jack didn't go on into Wyoming to hunt after all. He changed his mind when he saw the troops. He sent a courier back with the news. Tono says the camps are in an uproar over it."

Meeker smiled faintly. Then his expression changed and his face turned grave. He said, "I suppose I have mixed feelings over the coming of the troops. In a way I'm glad, because when they arrive we'll all feel more secure. But I'm sorry about it, too. Their coming will mean the end of everything I've tried to do."

"Maybe nobody is ever going to make farmers out of the Utes," Dave said. "Maybe it just isn't natural."

Meeker shook his head forcefully. "They've got to be farmers! They've got to be, because it's the only way they can survive! Why do you think I've been so harsh with them? Because I like to be? I'm not a harsh man, Dave, and I'm not ordinarily as stubborn as I've been of late. But I know time is running out for the Utes. They've got this reservation now, but they won't have it long. Every edition of the Denver newspapers carries the slogan, 'The Utes must go.' The people of Colorado are greedy for this land, and they'll have it before many more years have passed. I wanted the Utes to be self-supporting before that time arrived. I wanted to be able to show the government how they were making use of this land here at the agency."

Dave asked, "Isn't the reservation supposed to be theirs forever? Doesn't a treaty say it's theirs?"

Meeker smiled bitterly. "That's right, Dave, but we have broken every treaty we've ever made with the Indians, just as soon as we needed the Indians' land. And if those troops come here, it's the beginning of the end. I'm sorry I sent for them now. I wish I could send them back. If the Utes should fight them . . ." His voice trailed off.

Dave said, "Mr. Meeker, if the Indians fight the troops, they won't let us alone. They'll attack us, too."

Meeker shook his head. "They won't attack us, Dave. We are their friends."

Dave stared at him unbelievingly. The evidence of violence was here. Shad Price had been attacked. Meeker himself had been manhandled. Ute Jack had threatened Meeker with death right here in this very room. Yet Meeker would not believe the facts. Even when Tono warned how great the danger was, Meeker still would not listen.

Dave backed toward the door. Meeker had a distant expression on his face as if he had deliberately turned his thoughts to other things. Dave knew he would never convince Meeker that they ought to leave. And besides, it already was too late. It would be more dangerous to try to escape from the reservation without escort than it would be to remain.

For the moment Meeker seemed to have forgotten that Dave was in the room. A slight frown was on his forehead now. Dave slipped out quietly, taking care not to slam the screen door. He walked back to the woodpile where he had been working and picked up the saw, but for a moment he didn't resume his work. He stared at the Indian villages, thinking they seemed so peaceful. How could anything happen when everything was as quiet as it was now?

Dave began to saw wood again, working a good deal faster than he had before. Josie found relief from her fear in hard work. Maybe he could, too.

But in spite of himself, his mind kept returning to the problem. And occasionally he glanced fearfully in the direction of the Indian villages.

At supper everyone was unnaturally silent, and Josie Meeker's face was white and tense with strain. Flora Ellen Price spilled a pot of coffee and then burst into tears while she was cleaning it up.

Daylight faded, almost reluctantly, it seemed, as though in sympathy with the fearful whites. Before retiring, Meeker posted a guard on the warehouse in which the government's supplies for the Utes were stored. Dave thought how useless that would be if the Indians decided to break into the warehouse and take the goods.

He went to his room and tried to write a letter to his folks, but he had to give it up. His mind was in such a turmoil that he knew he'd be unable to write about his everyday work.

He blew out his lamp and sat by the window staring out into the night. A coyote pack quarreled shrilly on a nearby hill. A wolf howled in the distance. The drums kept beating, their tempo faster and somehow more barbaric and threatening tonight than on previous nights.

Finally he got into bed and slept, but it was an uneasy sleep from which the sound of drums and dancing Indians awakened him several times. He felt almost as tired when he got up in the morning as he had when he went to bed.

Breakfast was another silent and somber meal. Everyone knew by now that Jack had discovered the troops, and that he had not gone on to Wyoming as he had planned. But no one knew where he was right now.

After he finished eating, Dave followed the others out onto the porch. He sat on the steps, staring at the Indian villages. Then he saw dust along the road running north out of the valley, and a few moments later he was able to make out a mounted Indian brave thundering down the road into the villages at its foot.

Some of the agency men had been smoking and talking. All talk stopped and every eye was riveted on the road. Ten minutes after the first rider had disappeared into the villages, another brave appeared riding a different colored horse. He thundered up the road toward the north.

"Couriers," Price rumbled. "They're keeping the villages posted on what's going on. I wonder where the troops are now."

Nobody attempted a guess. After a while the men got up silently and went about their daily tasks. Tomorrow would be Sunday, Dave thought. He usually looked forward to Sunday because after church services he would go hunting or fishing with Tono. Or he would pitch horseshoes with the other agency employees.

This week he dreaded it because there would be no work to keep his mind occupied. And of course he would not go hunting or fishing with Tono. Suddenly he caught himself wondering if he would even be alive tomorrow.

He shook his head and told himself he would not think of that. Still, he wondered if the others felt as spooked as he did. He followed Shad Price to the milk house and asked, "Can I help you today?"

Shad peered at him and asked, "Why?"

Dave hesitated and felt his face turn hot. He said, "I guess I don't want to be alone. I guess I'm scared, if you want the truth."

Price cuffed his shoulder good-naturedly. "Sure, come on with me. Maybe the two of us can get that last load of dirt on the milk house roof."

Dave and Price worked side by side all day, talking only when it was necessary. Near quitting time Dave saw dust along the Rawlins road, and twenty minutes later Charlie Lowry rode in and dismounted in front of Meeker's house.

Lowry was the first white man from the outside world to reach the agency since Steele had left two weeks ago. Dave felt better when he saw him. At least the Utes had not closed the road to the agency.

The men stopped whatever they were doing and headed for Meeker's house. Lowry should be bringing mail, and he would also know if Jack's report of having seen troops at Bear River was true.

Meeker had come onto the porch, perhaps out of consideration for the employees. He knew their concern and he probably wanted to hear about the troops as much as anyone.

Lowry handed him a letter. He said, "I was given this on Fortification Creek, Mr. Meeker. That's about seventy-five miles north of here."

Meeker opened it. He looked at the men clustered in front of the porch. He said, "This is a letter to me from

Major Thornburgh written at his camp on Fortification Creek."

He cleared his throat and read aloud. "Sir: In obedience to instructions from the General of the Army, I am enroute to your agency, and expect to arrive there on the 29th instant, for the purpose of rendering you any assistance in my power, and to make arrests at your suggestions, and to hold as prisoners such of your Indians as you desire until investigations are made by your department. I have heard nothing definite from your agency for ten days and don't know what state of affairs exists; whether the Indians will leave at my approach or show resistance.

"I send this letter by Mr. Lowry, one of my guides, and desire you to communicate with me as soon as possible, giving me all the information in your power, in order that I may know what course to pursue. If practicable, meet me on the road at the earliest moment.

"Very respectfully, your obedient servant, T. T. Thornburgh, Major, Fourth Infantry, Commanding Expedition."

Meeker looked at Lowry. "How large a force does he command?"

"Three companies, sir. Plus about twenty-five civilians, scouts, packers, cooks, and the like."

"Have you seen Jack or any of his Indians?"

"Yes, sir. I saw Jack just outside the major's camp. I saw Sowerwick at Peck's store. He and Jack bought all the ammunition Peck had on hand, claiming it was for

66

their fall hunt in Wyoming. Ten thousand rounds, Mr. Meeker. Peck hasn't got a cartridge left in his store."

"Do you know when Jack bought the ammunition?"

"He bought it after he had seen Thornburgh at Bear River, so it sure ain't for no Wyoming hunt, Mr. Meeker. You can bet your hat on that."

"Anything else, Mr. Lowry?"

"Not that I think of right now. Are things all right here, Mr. Meeker?"

"So far they are. There's a lot of excitement in the villages, though. Drums beating every night, and Indians dancing and yelling so that a body can scarcely sleep. I'll be glad when the major gets here with his troops."

"Maybe it'd be better if he didn't bring the troops," Lowry said. "Maybe it'd be better if just the major came, along with maybe a civilian guide or two."

Meeker shook his head doubtfully. "I don't know. I don't know what the Indians might do in either case."

Lowry didn't seem to have anything else to say. Meeker said, "Come in, Mr. Lowry." He nodded at Dave. "Take care of Mr. Lowry's horse, Dave. Give him a good feed of oats."

"Yes, sir."

"And I'm doubling the guard on the warehouse tonight just in case. You and Frank Dresser will take the first guard, Dave, from dark until midnight. Mr. Price will take the second watch and pick someone to stand it with him."

"Yes, sir," Dave said and, picking up the reins of Lowry's horse, led him toward the stable.

Thornburgh and his troops were still seventy-five miles away. They couldn't get here before Monday night no matter how hard they tried.

After unsaddling and feeding Lowry's horse, Dave hurried out and washed for supper. At the boardinghouse, everyone was excited about the latest developments. Dave stared glumly toward the Ute villages. With troops coming, it was no wonder the Indians were scared. They knew what had happened before when soldiers moved onto reservations. Dave told himself he'd be scared, too, if he was a Ute. Troops could mean nothing but trouble for them.

CHAPTER
NINE

At dark Dave and Frank Dresser walked toward the warehouse. There was a stout padlock on the door. Meeker kept the key. Neither Dave nor Frank was armed. Dave had wanted to get his rifle, but Meeker had refused permission.

Dave supposed he was right in not letting the guards carry guns. They were not expected to defend the warehouse, only to give the alarm if the Indians tried breaking in. Dave realized that, with everyone so jumpy, someone might be shot accidentally. Still, he would have felt less nervous if he had a gun. He wondered where Tono was and what he was doing tonight.

Frank Dresser was about Dave's age, but certainly younger in appearance and attitude. He was really no more than a child, Dave thought. And tonight he was a mighty scared one. His teeth were chattering out loud by the time the two of them reached the warehouse.

Dave said, "I'm going to walk around and see that no windows have been broken or anything."

"I'll g-g-g-g-go with you," Frank stammered.

"All right, come on."

The two made a circle around the warehouse. Dave stopped at each window and checked to make sure the glass had not been broken. Back at the door again, Dave said, "Go over and sit against the wall, Frank. There's nothing to be scared of. All we're expected to do is give the alarm. It's all we can do."

"What does that mean? Are we supposed to yell or what?"

"We're supposed to run and wake Mr. Meeker and let him take care of it."

"I'm glad he wouldn't let us have guns," Frank said.

For a while Dave paced nervously back and forth. The drums were going full blast in the villages, sounding louder than they ever had before. Or maybe, Dave thought, it was only because the wind was blowing toward the agency from the villages. He knew that the wind carried sounds and magnified them. This seemed to be more true at night than in the daytime.

He wondered where Major Thornburgh and his command were now. It had probably taken Charlie Lowry at least twelve hours to make the ride from Fortification Creek. He must have left at dawn or earlier to have made it to the agency when he had. Thornburgh, then, would be a day's march closer by now.

Dave wondered how far three companies of soldiers could travel in a day. They would have a lot of wagons and mules, and the roads north of the agency certainly weren't very good. In fact, they were little more than trails. The soldiers could cover no more ground than the slowest wagon. Dave doubted they could travel any more than twenty miles a day.

That meant it was almost a four-day journey between Fortification Creek and the agency. Tonight the troops would still be three days away, or almost sixty miles.

Frank's teeth were still chattering noisily. Dave felt sorry for him and wished he could send him away. But he couldn't. And suddenly it dawned on him what the reason was for having two guards. If they were jumped, one or the other might be able to get away and give the alarm.

He smiled faintly to himself. He didn't know what Meeker could do about it even if the Utes did decide to break into the warehouse and take the annuity goods.

Suddenly he heard a twig snap somewhere out in the darkness. He froze, listening intently. A chill ran up his spine and spread down his arms until he could feel the goose bumps on his skin. Someone was out there, and it could only be an Indian.

Frank's voice was thin and scared, a mere whisper as he said, "What was that?"

Scarcely had he spoken when suddenly Indians appeared out of the darkness on all sides of the two boys. Dave backed against the warehouse door. Frank said, "D-D-Dave? Hadn't one of us ought to run for Mr. Meeker?"

Dave said thinly, "Too late. Stay put, Frank." To the shadowy Indians he said, trying not to sound as scared as he felt, "What are you doing here? What do you want?"

"Want blankets. Break down door and take. You get out of way or you get hurt." It was Ute Jack's voice.

Dave hesitated. He knew he couldn't stop them. He knew Meeker couldn't stop them either. If he tried, it might start the violence everybody was trying to avoid. On the other hand, Dave hadn't been put on guard just to turn the warehouse over to the Indians. If they got the blankets, they'd trade them for whiskey at Peck's store. Full of whiskey they would be even meaner and more dangerous than they already were.

Dave said, "You can't get in. I've got a gun here and I'll use it if you force me to."

Frank's voice was a terrified wail. "Dave . . ."

Jack said, "Get out of the way. Heap quick."

Dave said, "Nothing doing. If you want in this warehouse, you get Mr. Meeker to give you the key."

"We break lock." Jack's voice was still sullen and angry, but Dave had the feeling that Jack was wavering. He said, "You try to break this lock and I'll put a bullet in you."

He knew it was too dark for them to tell whether he had a gun or not. He was glad they couldn't see how pale he was and that his knees were trembling. Holding his breath, he waited for them to rush him, or shoot him down right where he stood. He wanted to turn and run, but something kept him rooted to the spot.

At last Jack grunted, with grudging admiration in his voice, "You heap good young brave for white man. No shoot. We go." He turned and disappeared into the darkness and the others followed him.

Dave was cold from head to foot. His whole body was shaking and his teeth were chattering. He supposed Frank was just as scared.

But the Indians had gone. He leaned against the warehouse until his trembling began to subside. When he could trust himself to speak, he said to Frank, "I don't want you to tell anybody about what happened. Do you understand? They didn't get in the warehouse and that's all that matters as far as we're concerned. Telling what happened will only make the trouble worse."

Dresser didn't say anything. Dave wondered if he, himself, would be able to keep quiet about what had happened here tonight. It would be hard not to brag just a little bit. He had faced up to Ute Jack and won. But he knew telling would only make matters worse between Meeker and the Indians when the troops arrived.

At midnight he sent Frank to wake Shad Price, and ten minutes later Price approached with another man whom Dave did not recognize in the darkness. He hurried back to his room with Frank running beside him trying to keep up.

The drums were still going, but the shrill cries of the Indians had dwindled away and died. He didn't think he could sleep after the tension of standing guard and facing down Ute Jack, but he got into bed. He fell asleep almost instantly.

Dave slept later than usual on Sunday morning. It was seven when he woke. He dressed rapidly and ran to the boardinghouse, afraid he was too late for breakfast. The others had finished eating except for Frank, Shad, and Arthur Thompson, the man who had stood the second guard with Shad.

The four sat down at the long table, and Josie Meeker brought them a platter of bacon and scrambled eggs a few minutes later. She had baked fresh biscuits and brought another platter heaped high with them.

Dave pitched in hungrily. Josie went to the door and stood staring somberly at the Indian villages, from which plumes of wood smoke rose into the still morning air.

Turning her head, she said, "Someone's coming."

Immediately Price rose from the table and went to the door. The others followed. Squinting against the brilliant morning sun, Dave saw a rider pounding along the dusty road toward the agency. He looked like an Indian, but when the man pulled his horse to a halt before Meeker's house, Dave saw that he was not a Ute, but a half-breed, probably one of Thornburgh's interpreters or scouts.

Meeker had undoubtedly been watching his approach. Now he stood in front of his house waiting for the man. Josie said, "I'll go find out what it's all about. You men finish eating."

Reluctantly Dave returned to the table and sat down. He finished eating, filled with a dark foreboding. He was oppressed this morning with the conviction that events were marching toward sure violence.

He had finished eating and was drinking the last of his coffee when Josie returned. She stood in the doorway with the sun at her back and said, "It's a man named Henry Jim who is an interpreter for Thornburgh's command. He says Lowry reached Major Thornburgh. He brought a message from the major saying he would camp on Milk Creek and come on to the agency with only five soldiers, guided by Mr. Eskridge, who as you know left here a short time ago for a vacation with his family in Greeley. Father wants one of you to go into the Ute villages and find Chief Jack and bring him here. Father wants Jack to know that Thornburgh is not bringing his whole command."

Dave realized Josie was looking straight at him. She said, "Dave, you'd have the best chance of finding Jack without getting into trouble. The Utes are used to seeing you in their villages. Will you go?"

She was right, Dave thought as he got up. He was the only one who could go into the Ute villages safely. The Indians were used to seeing him there with Tono. He said, "Sure, I'll go?"

The way she looked at him made him glad he hadn't hesitated or let anyone know he was afraid. He got his hat and started down the road, staying in plain sight of the villages so that no Indian would get the idea he was trying to spy on them.

Several times he was tempted to turn and look back toward the agency, but he didn't. He was tempted, too, to run, or at least lengthen his stride, but he kept rigid control of himself, walking with his usual gait, just as if he were going to visit Tono. He had never felt more alone.

Dave knew exactly where Ute Jack's tepee was, but he didn't turn from the road into the villages until he was opposite it. Even so, he felt his nerves tighten with each step, half expecting a gunshot to ring out or an arrow to whiz toward him and bury itself in his flesh.

Most of the Indians he passed glared at him sullenly, but he didn't pause until he reached Jack's tepee. He called, "Chief Jack, are you there?"

He waited a moment, and when there was no answer he lifted the tepee flap and looked inside. Jack sat cross-legged on the floor in front of the fire. There were several other Indians with him, including Sowerwick, Douglas, and the fat, perpetually scowling Colorow. Plainly Dave had interrupted some kind of council of the chiefs.

Dave cleared his throat and said, "Mr. Meeker would like to see you, Chief Jack. He has received a message from Major Thornburgh."

Jack scowled at him, but he did not reply. Dave realized he had done all he could. He certainly couldn't make the chief do anything he didn't want to. He backed out of the lodge into the sunshine again.

Once more he had a strong impulse to run, but he forced himself to walk slowly back to the road. When he reached it, he glanced behind him. The four chiefs were standing in front of Ute Jack's lodge arguing heatedly. He went on, hurrying along the road toward the agency.

He was about a quarter mile from Meeker's house when he heard the thunder of hooves coming toward him. Turning his head, he saw Jack pounding toward him on a paint pony. The chief rode arrogantly in the middle of the road and Dave had to jump for the ditch at the side as he thundered past. Jack rode right to the steps of Meeker's house and flung himself from his horse.

From a distance of two hundred yards or so, Dave saw Meeker come out of the house accompanied by the half-breed interpreter, Henry Jim. He did run now, wanting to hear what was said.

He could see Josie, Flora, and the men clustered in front of the boardinghouse, staring at Chief Jack, Meeker, and the interpreter. As Dave ran up, he heard Meeker saying, ". . . soldiers are not coming to the agency, Chief Jack. I thought you would want to know. Major Thornburgh is coming in alone, accompanied by four or five soldiers and a guide."

"Why Meeker send for soldiers?" Jack demanded.

Meeker looked aggrieved. "You know what Johnson did to me. You know your people have been dancing for more than two weeks and have refused to work. You also know that Mr. Price and Dave there were fired upon while trying to plow."

Jack glared at Meeker for a moment and then said sullenly, "It good thing Thornburgh no bring soldiers here. Jack make plan for them."

"What plan?" Meeker asked with concern.

"Jack ambush soldiers if soldiers cross Milk Creek. Soldiers no supposed to come on reservation. Utes make big war if they do."

Meeker turned his head and looked at Henry Jim as if telling him to pass on this bit of information to

Thornburgh when he returned. Looking at Jack again, he said, "That would be very foolish. You can't fight the government. You will lose everything if you try."

Jack's scowl seemed to be frozen on his dark face. He looked at Meeker and then turned his head to stare for a moment at Dave. Abruptly he turned and strode to his horse. He did not look back at either Meeker or Henry Jim, but mounted and thundered back down the road in the direction of the villages.

Meeker, white and shaken, looked at Dave and smiled wearily. "Thank you for fetching him, Dave. It was a courageous act."

"It wasn't anything much," Dave said, embarrassed by the unexpected praise.

Meeker turned and went back into the house. Henry Jim led his horse toward the stable. Dave walked slowly toward the group idling in front of the boardinghouse. It was almost time for him to get cleaned up for church services, he thought, and wondered what kind of sermon Meeker would preach today.

CHAPTER
TEN

The rest of the day was as quiet as Dave had expected, but he hadn't expected Sunday to seem so ominous. No one mentioned it, but he thought the others felt the grimness, too. It was, he told himself, the quiet before the storm.

The villages were quiet also, despite the fact that few of the Utes were Christian, and still fewer kept the Sabbath as white men did. Dave decided they were holding councils, trying to decide what they should do.

The Utes knew that Thornburgh was on the road with three companies. And it was common knowledge that Captain Dodge and his troop of black cavalry were in Middle Park, to the east, and could be at the White River Agency in two days if necessary.

On the other hand, the Utes would be considering what Meeker had told Jack this morning — that Thornburgh was coming on alone with an escort of only four or five troopers.

The question was whether they would believe what Meeker had said. They probably thought it was a trap. Indians were suspicious of the things white men said under such circumstances, and with justification.

They'd been lied to and cheated in every dealing they'd ever had with the whites.

Dave thought about this when he went to his room in the afternoon to write another letter home. He mentioned the danger because he knew his folks would have heard some news of the unrest, even as far away as Greeley. But he tried to minimize it by keeping his doubts and worries out of the letter.

Once more Greeley seemed a much better place to live than it had six months ago. Thinking of it made Dave feel warm and safe. But as far as he was concerned, Greeley was a million miles away. He wondered if he would ever see it again.

He tried to read, but had a difficult time keeping his mind on the book. It was *Pilgrim's Progress*, one of his favorites, but this was not a day for reading. Finally he put it away and went outside to sit with the others in the shade of one of the agency buildings.

The afternoon dragged on. Price's two small children played as if they didn't have a care in the world. At least they had nothing to fear, Dave thought. The Indians loved them and, even if they didn't, they would not hurt children, Indian or white. Eventually both of them got tired and cross, and Flora Ellen took them in and put them down for their naps.

Supper was another quiet meal, with nobody having much to say. Everyone seemed to be waiting, straining for the first drum to begin its throbbing cadence, for the first shrill, distant cry to break the silence of the villages.

The sun went down in a bloodred sky, and the purple of dusk moved across the primitive land. At last the first drum throbbed, and moments later a shrill chorus of cries came drifting down the breeze, sounding like coyotes quarreling over a kill.

The agency employees sat in the dusk. Occasionally someone would slap a mosquito. Two of the men smoked pipes and the fragrant smoke gave Dave a pleasant feeling of companionship.

The sounds increased in intensity in the villages, but tonight, Dave thought uneasily, they seemed different. Always before there had been the drums and the shrill cries, but tonight Dave caught something else, something that sounded like the roar of a crowd at a horse race.

Price stood up and stared through the gathering darkness. "Puttin' on a war dance, sounds like," he said.

"What does that mean?" Fred Shepard asked. "That they're fixin' to attack the agency?"

"Not likely the agency," Price answered. "My guess would be Major Thornburgh's three companies."

"They'll be a sorry bunch of Indians if they do that," Shepard said.

Price puffed thoughtfully on his pipe for a moment. "I wouldn't be too sure of that. They're well armed with repeating Winchesters, and they ain't like the plains tribes who don't take care of their rifles and don't usually shoot real straight. These boogers can knock a squirrel out of a tree at fifty yards."

Shepard nodded agreement. "They got ten thousand rounds of ammunition at Peck's store a couple of days ago. Thornburgh might be in trouble if the Utes jump him before he gets here. I expect you're right, Shad."

"Eskridge is a fool if he comes back," William Post said. "He had a chance to get clear out of this. Believe me, if I'd had the chance, I'd have taken it."

Price took his pipe out of his mouth. "My wife's just about scared to death. I wish I could get her and the kids out, but I reckon it's actually safer here than it would be on the road. If Thornburgh does come with five soldiers, I'm going to try to get him to take her back to Rawlins with him."

"I don't suppose Mrs. Meeker and Josephine would go, would they?" Post asked.

Price shook his head. "I doubt it, if Meeker stays, and I figure he will. But Flora's different. She's got the kids to think of."

The sounds from the direction of the villages had increased in intensity. Dave stood up and peered into the darkness. For an instant he wondered if Tono had painted his face and was participating in the war dance. He felt disloyal at the thought, because he knew that Tono didn't believe in the old, barbaric ways, or that there had to be warfare between the Indians and the whites.

Dave heard the screen door of Meeker's house slam and glanced in that direction. The agent had come out onto the porch. Illuminated from the doorway behind him, he stood peering at the villages, the fires, the wildly dancing figures. A moment later Mrs. Meeker came through the door and stood beside him.

An unaccountable sadness touched Dave as he thought about them. They were good people, both of them. Meeker was honest and sincere in his desire to help the Indians. Mrs. Meeker apparently had no opinions of her own. She merely loved her husband and was loyal to him. Yet Meeker had failed, and because of this he might die within the next few days. Mrs. Meeker, who had done nothing at all, might die with him.

Dave shook his head angrily. He wished he could stop thinking about death. He was probably just letting his imagination run away with him. Nobody was going to die. But Tono's warning kept coming back into his mind.

He went to his room and without lighting the lamp got into bed. He stared into the darkness gloomily and listened to the throbbing of the drums. He had thought that he would get used to hearing them, but he hadn't. Stiff and tense, he lay there for a long time before he finally went to sleep.

Dave was eating breakfast the next morning when Meeker came into the boardinghouse. He looked haggard and gray. His shoulders were slumped and he had not yet shaved, a fact that made him look even more haggard.

Dave glanced around as Meeker said, "I would like to see you for a minute when you have finished eating, Dave."

"Yes, sir. I'll be there right away."

Meeker left and Dave finished his breakfast hastily. He wiped his mouth on the back of his hand and hurried out through the door, cramming his hat on his head. He wondered if Meeker wanted him to go into the Ute villages again and found himself hoping not.

Meeker was waiting in his office. He had just finished writing a letter and was sealing the envelope flap as Dave entered the room. He glanced up.

"Henry Jim left here without me seeing him," Meeker said. "I have a message I want to send to Thornburgh at once. I talked to Douglas early this morning and he has agreed to accompany me to meet Thornburgh on the road. Another Ute will go with us, though I don't know yet who it will be.

"I would like you to find Tono and get him to accompany you. I want this letter delivered to the major. I am warning him to be on guard because, while Douglas seems peacefully inclined, I can't say the same for Jack. Jack claims he intends to attack the major if he leads his command across Milk Creek."

He paused a moment while he addressed the envelope in his precise, meticulous hand, and went on, "I do not know whether Jack will attack the major and his five-man escort, but I think he should be warned. If you leave immediately, and push your horse hard, you should manage to reach Thornburgh before he can cross Milk Creek. Take the best horse in the stable. The bay gelding, Rex, is probably the one."

"Yes, sir." Dave said.

Meeker's smile was meant to be encouraging, but it seemed more like the grimace of a tired and frightened old man. He said, "Be careful, Dave. I am asking you to do something dangerous. That is why I should like Tono to go with you. I know how close you two have become."

Meeker stared at Dave so long that he began to feel uncomfortable. At least the agent said gravely, "You and Tono have unwittingly found the thing for which I have searched so long and hard, friendship and harmony between Indian and white. I hope you two will be able to remain friends during the coming days. It is a sad thing that we older people cannot achieve what you boys have."

Dave said uneasily, "I guess I'd better go, Mr. Meeker. I'll have to find Tono and I don't know where he is."

Meeker nodded. "Yes, Dave. Go on." He handed Dave the letter and Dave turned and hurried out of the office.

He was excited at the prospect of carrying a message to Major Thornburgh. His heart thumped as he thought how dangerous it was, but, dangerous or not, it was better than waiting while the hours dragged by.

He ran to the stable and saddled the gelding Meeker had suggested. Rex was a young horse and certainly the fastest one at the agency. Dave had ridden him several times, but he still was not sure how the animal would hold up on a ride as long as this one would probably be.

Before he had finished saddling up, Josie Meeker came into the stable, a canvas sack of food in one hand, a blanket roll in the other. Dave tied them behind the saddle.

"Take a sack of oats for your horse, Dave," Josie said. "You've got a hard ride ahead of you."

"Uh-huh." He took a gunnysack, filled it a quarter full of oats, and tied it on the side opposite the sack of food. Then he swung himself into the saddle.

He looked down at her for a moment, all the uncertainty he felt showing in his face. He was going to do a man's job, but he was not a man. Not yet. He had succeeded in doing several things in the last few weeks that he could not have done before leaving Greeley. He would succeed in this, too, he told himself. He had to.

Josie seemed to understand and had the good sense not to say anything. Dave whirled the horse and rode away, digging his heels into the animal's sides to make him gallop.

The pace gave him a feeling of exhilaration that dispelled his uncertainty. It was good to be riding a fast horse again, to feel the wind in his face and have the sensation that the whole world was flashing by. He raced down the road, heading for Tono's lodge.

He was so conscious of the letter in his pocket that it seemed to burn through to his skin. He might still be scared a little, he thought, but he was proud that Meeker had showed such trust in him.

Halfway to Tono's lodge, he turned his head and stared back at the agency. The familiar buildings looked snug and secure. They had been home for quite a while, and he could not bear to think of anything happening to them. He could see people moving about, dwarfed by distance and unrecognizable. They were his friends, and he could not bear to think of anything happening to them.

If he failed to reach Thornburgh in time to keep him from crossing Milk Creek with his command, then the Utes would certainly attack the three companies. They would probably attack the agency at the same time. That was reason enough to deliver the letter, he told himself. The thought sent a prickle down his spine, and with it came the realization that he had never attempted anything as important as this before.

There seemed to be fewer lodges in the villages than there had been yesterday, when he had come to fetch Ute Jack. Suddenly Dave realized that many of the lodges were gone. The places where they had stood were bare, but their outlines were clearly visible on the ground.

It was another ominous sign, Dave thought uneasily. When Indians evacuate their women and children, it usually means they are getting ready for a fight.

He found Tono's tepee. Tono's uncle and his two wives were in the process of taking it down and loading it onto a travois. Tono was helping. As Dave approached, he glanced up and frowned.

"Is your family leaving?" Dave asked.

Tono nodded, almost sullenly, it seemed to Dave. Tono said, "They are going south to Grand River for a while. Nobody knows what the soldiers will do when they reach this place. My uncle believes they will be safer near Grand River."

Dave didn't blame Tono's family for leaving. "Mr. Meeker has given me a message to take to Major Thornburgh," Dave said. "He asked me to get you to ride with me."

Tono looked doubtful and Dave immediately understood the reason for his doubt. He said quickly, "I know what is in the message, Tono. It is not a request to Major Thornburgh to bring his command to the agency. It is only a message saying Mr. Meeker will meet the major and a few soldiers and a guide along the road. Meeker is to bring Douglas and another Indian. He hopes to bring about a settlement by getting Douglas and Major Thornburgh to talk."

Tono's expression relaxed. He looked at his uncle, a middle-aged, heavy-chested man. His uncle nodded, apparently giving permission for his nephew to go.

Tono swung to the back of his horse, a stocky pinto, and trotted toward the road. Dave followed, staying as close as possible. Tono guided his horse straight up the slope of the first ridge, angling toward the road that led to Milk Creek and to Rawlins beyond.

Dave rode a few yards behind him. It was plain that Tono didn't want to talk. It was also plain that he was in even more of a hurry than Dave was.

Dave wondered why, but he didn't have to wonder very long. No sooner had the ridgetop hidden them from the White River valley and the agency buildings than a Ute warrior galloped along the slope to intercept them.

Tono had only enough time to say, "Let me do the talking, Dave," before the Ute pulled his horse to a halt directly in front of them.

CHAPTER
ELEVEN

Dave recognized the Ute as a minor chief named Badger. He had seen Badger with Jack several times, usually scowling as fiercely as he was right now. The Ute put several rapid questions to Tono in their own tongue.

Tono replied almost as rapidly. Dave felt his uneasiness grow as the conversation continued. He wished he knew what they were saying. The letter felt so bulky and heavy in his pocket that he felt Badger was bound to notice it. He wondered what he should do if Badger demanded that he surrender it. Should he resist or try to get away?

Tono moved his horse closer to Dave and said in a low voice, "He wanted to know where we were going. He wanted me to tell him what was in the message, so I told him it was an offer by Mr. Meeker to meet Thornburgh and a few soldiers and a guide along the road. I said it was not a request to Thornburgh to bring in his whole command, but I do not think he believed me."

"That's right," Dave said. "What can we say to make him believe it?"

Tono shook his head, troubled. He didn't answer. Instead, he said, "I hope you told me the truth, Dave. He can't read, and he does not know English, so he could not tell what was in the letter if he took it away from you. But he says he is going with us. As soon as he can find someone who can read, he will take the letter away from you and get them to read it to him."

Dave said honestly, "I told you what Meeker told me, Tono. I didn't lie and I'm sure he didn't. He wouldn't send me off with a message and lie to me about what it said."

"No, I do not suppose he would." Tono left Dave's side and rode closer to the scowling Ute. He spoke to him rapidly and what he said seemed to satisfy Badger, at least for the time. His scowl faded slightly. He made a gesture to indicate that Tono and Dave could proceed. Tono rode down to the road and Dave followed. Badger fell in behind them. Glancing around, Dave saw that there was still suspicion and doubt in the man's black eyes.

They rode this way for several miles. Dave felt as though Badger was staring steadily at his back. Uneasiness grew in him. It wasn't helped by Tono's expression when he turned his head to look at Dave. Tono was plainly worried and more than a little scared.

Dave asked himself what would happen if they didn't find anyone who could read. If they didn't, Badger wouldn't be able to have the message read to him. Unable to find out what the letter contained, he'd probably demand that Dave give it to him so he could destroy it. He would still suspect that Dave knew what it contained and could deliver the message verbally, so he might try to prevent Dave from going on.

The thought sent a cold chill running down Dave's spine. The Ute might try to kill him, and if Tono intervened he might kill Tono, too.

When he had a chance, Dave searched Tono's face surreptitiously. He was ashamed of himself for thinking it, but he caught himself wondering if Tono *would* help. Tono turned his head, caught Dave's glance, and frowned.

Dave felt his face grow hot with shame. He knew that Tono would give his life trying to fight Badger off. And he wouldn't be able to help Tono very much if a fight did develop. He was unarmed. Moreover, although Tono had his rifle and a knife, he would be no match for an older, stronger, fully grown brave like Badger. There could be only one end to such a fight. Dave and Tono would both die.

The road dipped down into a wide, shallow valley. Here on the north side of White River valley there was little timber. The ground was covered with sagebrush. Clumps of flaming serviceberry and tangled patches of scrub oak grew here and there. Once a deer bounded ahead of them until he was lost to sight behind a ridge half a mile away.

The sun was warm, the land very dry. Dust from the hooves of the three horses rose in a cloud over the road behind them. The smell of sagebrush crushed by their passage was pungent and pleasant in the air.

Badger, riding behind Dave, began to mutter angrily to himself. It seemed that each mile they traveled made him more suspicious about the message. This, in turn, seemed to increase his frustration over his inability to find out what it said.

Tono was riding about a dozen yards in front of Dave. He didn't turn, but occasionally he cocked his head slightly to one side as though trying to hear what Badger was muttering. Obviously he was able to catch some of it. But he said nothing and did not look at Dave.

If only the two of them could get away from Badger, Dave thought. But it was impossible. Unless . . . unless they split up. If they did that, Badger would most certainly follow Dave. If he could somehow slip the message to Tono beforehand and ask him to take it to Thornburgh, then Tono could make a run for it while Badger was chasing Dave.

Just thinking about what would happen to him when Badger caught up with him sent prickles running down his spine again. No, he decided, the situation was not desperate enough yet to take that kind of chance. They would probably encounter someone before long. Once the message was read to Badger, he would turn back and let Tono and Dave go on.

Badger continued to mutter angrily. Once, when Tono did look back at the other Ute, Dave saw the frightened expression in his eyes. As long as he had known Tono, he had never seen him look like this before.

The time dragged until it seemed more than Dave could bear. It was worse than waiting back at the agency. Now the danger was very close in the person of the unpredictable Badger, and this increased the tension until Dave felt as if his nerves were singing.

He could not do anything except keep on riding. They went through a small pocket of timber on the north slope of the hill. When they reached the ridgetop, Dave stared longingly at the horizon ahead, at the endless hills stretching away almost to infinity. He wondered whether he would ever see the blue-clad soldiers under Thornburgh, or whether they would find his body lying where Badger had killed him.

He shook his head impatiently. It was hard not to be scared and hard not to think about the danger he was in. But thinking about it wasn't going to do him any good. It would only paralyze him so that, when the time for action came, he'd be too slow to do whatever had to be done.

They came to a small stream at the bottom of the next ravine. Badger stopped his horse and let him drink. He didn't seem worried about the boys getting away from him. Dave wondered why he was so confident and decided that Badger knew there were so many Ute braves ahead of them. If the boys did get away, they would run into more trouble than they were in now.

Dave had caught up with Tono. So that Badger wouldn't see him talking to Tono, he dismounted and pretended to be tightening his cinch. Without turning his head, he said in a low tone, "Tell me something, Tono, and tell me the truth. Is he going to kill me?"

Tono was staring north, his head turned away from Badger when he spoke. "That's what he's been muttering about. He doesn't believe the message says what you told him. He thinks Meeker is asking Thornburgh to bring his whole command to the agency. If that happens, he thinks the whole tribe will be sent to Indian Territory. He's been hesitating because he doesn't want to start the trouble by killing the first white man, but he won't wait much longer."

"What are we going to do?"

"I have been trying to think of something, Dave. If I could put a gun in his back and hold him long enough for you to get away —"

"He'll kill you, Tono."

"Maybe not."

"You'd be an outcast from your tribe. They'd say you betrayed them whether you did or not."

"That is better than you being killed."

"I can't let you do it," Dave said desperately. "I won't let you do it."

"You haven't got anything to say about it, Dave," Tono said, his voice determined. "You cannot stop me. When I yell for you to run, you run. I probably will not be able to hold him more than half an hour at the most. You'll have to stay ahead of him until you reach the soldiers. Watch out that you don't run into some more of my people."

Dave finished with his cinch and swung into the saddle. His throat felt dry and his eyes burned. Tono was willing to risk his life for him. And he had doubted his friend earlier.

CHAPTER
TWELVE

As the hours passed, Badger lapsed into sullen silence. The road wound northward like a dusty snake crawling through the brushy, barren hills. Half a dozen times Tono tried to drop behind so that he would be able to maneuver into a position where he could disarm Badger. But each time the big Ute spoke to him harshly, and Tono moved into the lead again.

The sun was almost directly overhead when Badger finally gave the word to stop. Dave dismounted in the shade of a clump of cottonwoods whose brilliant, waxy yellow leaves rustled softly above him. He loosened his saddle cinch, then dropped the reins, and the horse moved away and began to graze.

Tono and Badger did the same, allowing the horses to move into the cottonwoods to graze. The grass here was long and dry. Dave wondered how far they were from the reservation boundary at Milk Creek, and if they would meet Thornburgh or any other whites before reaching there. He doubted it, but he knew it was possible.

Dave walked to his horse and got the sack Josie had given him. Returning, he studied Tono's face, trying to read its expression, trying to decide if this was where Tono would try to overcome Badger.

Tono's face was even more expressionless than usual, and Dave decided that his friend *would* try to get the drop on Badger here.

Josie had packed a dozen pieces of cold fried chicken, along with a number of biscuits left over from yesterday. There were also some molasses cookies. Although noon was more than an hour off, Dave opened the sack and spread the food out on the ground. He said, "Tell him to help himself, Tono. When he bends over to do it, maybe you can get the drop on him."

Tono spoke to Badger in the Indian tongue. Badger, who already had his eyes on the food, moved toward it, watching Dave suspiciously as he did. He licked his lips and swallowed, then squatted beside the sack and reached out to pick up a piece of fried chicken.

Tono had moved silently so that he stood behind Badger. Now he jabbed his rifle into the other Ute's back and spoke to him sharply. Tono looked at Dave and said, "Get his gun."

Carefully Dave moved in from the side. Badger had put his rifle on the ground beside him when he squatted beside the food. Dave, getting no closer than necessary, grabbed the gun and ducked back out of Badger's reach.

Badger's face was contorted with rage. His eyes, narrowed and black, gave Dave the shivers. Badger started to turn, but Tono snapped something at him and jabbed him again savagely in the back with the muzzle of his gun. He said, "Get started, Dave. Drop his rifle in the middle of the road after you've gone about half a mile."

Dave ran to his horse, tightened the cinch, and led the animal back to where Tono and Badger were. Badger was still squatted in front of the food, but he seemed to have lost any interest in eating.

"I can't leave you like this, Tono," Dave said. "He'll kill you when you let him go."

"No, he won't," Tono said. "He's pretty mad right now, but he'll cool off."

"Why don't you tie him up and come with me?"

Tono glanced at him as if Dave should know the answer to that question. He said, "Because I am a Ute, not a white like you."

Dave opened his mouth to argue, then decided not to press the point any further. Tono was right, of course. He was an Indian in spite of the years he had lived among the whites. He'd be just as lost now if he returned to the white people as Dave would be if he went to live with the Utes.

Reluctantly he turned his horse away. He had been terrified of Badger and now he was escaping from him, but he was not as elated as he had thought he would be. He had a terrifying feeling that this was the last time he would see his friend.

He halted his horse impulsively and swung around in the saddle. He looked back as he said, "Thanks sounds pretty weak, Tono."

"It is enough," Tono said quickly. "Now go. Ride hard and fast, because I don't know how long I will be

98

able to hold Badger here. If any other Utes should pass this way, they would make me release him and he would come after you."

Dave raised a hand in a farewell gesture and dug his heels into the horse's sides. The animal broke into a gallop. Dave kept drumming with his heels until the bay gelding broke into a steady run.

He rode at this hard pace for what he judged to be half a mile. Then he slowed the horse and dropped Badger's rifle in the road. Maybe, while Badger was coming after his gun, Tono would be able to get away, he thought.

Then Dave shook his head. Tono hadn't been thinking about getting away. He'd acted like a man prepared to take his medicine for what he had done. He'd accompany Badger back to the villages and take whatever punishment was given him.

Suddenly Dave understood something about his mission to Thornburgh. Meeker had certainly wanted his message delivered, but that had not been his only motive in sending Dave and Tono to deliver it. He could have sent one of the older men at the agency just as easily.

Meeker had wanted both Dave and Tono to be far from the agency when the trouble broke. He had tried to save both their lives and friendship by sending them away. And Tono had risked his own life to save his friend. Dave felt tears burning in his eyes as he drummed his heels more insistently on the horse's sides. He probably would never have a chance to repay Tono.

As he rode, he kept watch on the slopes rising from the road ahead of him. And he listened for hoofbeats on the road behind. Not that he had any specific plan in case he did hear sounds of pursuit. He'd just have to force the bay to run faster than ever and hope he reached the troops before his pursuer overtook him.

It was well into the afternoon before he stopped. His horse was lathered and trembling. Dave knew that he had to rest the gelding or the animal would lie down and die. Dismounting beside a small stream, he let the horse drink sparingly and then dragged him forcibly away from the water. He led him off the road into a thick clump of willows, removed the saddle, and rubbed him down with the soggy saddle blanket.

When Dave finished, he led the horse back to the stream and let him drink again. He would have to allow the animal to travel at a slower pace for the rest of the afternoon or he would finish his journey to Milk Creek on foot.

He saddled the bay again. He had his foot in the stirrup when he heard a strange sound drifting along on the light breeze that was blowing toward him from the north. It was a familiar sound, or seemed to be, but it had no place out here in the wilderness, particularly at this time of year. It sounded the way it had in Greeley last Fourth of July — like firecrackers going off, singly and in strings.

Then he realized what it really was: the sound of guns, the steady cracking of many rifles. It couldn't be anything else.

His message was too late. Thornburgh must have crossed Milk Creek and led his command on south toward the agency. The Utes, as Jack had threatened, had attacked the soldiers the minute they crossed the boundary.

Dave stood there, frozen, one foot in the stirrup, the other on the ground. He stared ahead into the timber, stared toward the sound of gunfire, and then turned his head to look back in the direction from which he had come.

He could not go back. Badger was there, and even if he worked his way past Badger, there was no safety at the agency. On the other hand, he did not see how he could get through the Indians ahead of him. Jack and Colorow would certainly have led hundreds of Ute warriors from their villages to stop the major's troops.

In any case, he certainly could not stay here. Indians were going to be traveling back and forth along this road in steady streams, going for reinforcements, ammunition, and food, and taking news of the battle back to the villages.

Swiftly he swung into the saddle and reined his horse straight up the steep hillside to his left. He would have to reach Thornburgh. It was his only chance to survive, but he couldn't get to him by taking the road. His only chance would be to come from another direction, and even then he might blunder into some of the Indians.

After he had crossed the first ridge above the road, he traveled in ravines whenever possible. His hand holding the reins was shaking violently. He could feel his knees knocking against the horse's sides. Angrily he gripped the horse with his knees to make them stop trembling.

He was scared, but, doggone it, he had a right to be scared. A grown man like Shad Price would have been scared in a situation like this. These hills were alive with fighting Indians, and he was alone and unarmed. He remembered telling Shad after the shooting in the horse pasture that he was scared; Price had cuffed him on the shoulder and said, "You're not the only one."

Dave wondered whether he wouldn't be smart to leave his horse and continue afoot. He debated the question for several minutes before he shook his head. He decided against it, for the horse certainly gave him mobility and speed, which more than offset the increased risk of discovery. If he had to run, or if he had to make a dash through the Indian lines to reach the troops, the horse would be a necessity.

Now the sounds of gunfire were louder. Once he thought he smelled powder smoke on the breeze. As the crackling of rifle fire became louder, he traveled more cautiously. At last he dismounted, tied the horse, crept to the top of a low ridge, and peered into the valley below him.

He was still at least half a mile from the scene of battle. Between him and the place where Tornburgh's troops had made their stand there was a heavily timbered slope. The valley bottom lay beyond the timber, with Milk Creek a whitish-colored stream that wound along one side of it. The road, only a two-track affair at this point, roughly followed the course of the stream.

102

Dead horses were scattered around the soldiers' besieged position. With a shudder Dave saw what must be the bodies of several soldiers lying haphazardly in the fringe of the timber, white and naked, having been stripped of their uniforms by the Utes.

Dave felt cold. He had begun to shiver and his teeth were chattering uncontrollably. He looked down at his hands and clenched them to stop the trembling. Thornburgh's men were pinned down in a little grove of thin trees about 150 yards from the stream.

At least they were near water, Dave thought, and told himself that would be vital if the siege lasted any length of time. Some shelter was provided by their wagons and the bodies of their dead animals.

Dave remembered Captain Dodge and his company of black cavalry in Middle Park. But he could not even hope that Captain Dodge would be able to rescue Thornburgh's command. He could see hundreds of Ute braves surrounding the major's men. Even if Dodge came to their relief, both commands would be almost hopelessly outnumbered.

He wriggled back to where he had left the bay. He wanted desperately to make a wide circle and continue north toward Rawlins. There were two reasons why he did not.

First, he had a message to deliver to Major Thornburgh, and he would fail to do his duty if he didn't deliver it. Second, he was more afraid of giving in to his fear than he was of the Indians.

He untied the horse and mounted. He angled along the crest of the ridge until it seemed to him that the

103

firing was no more than a hundred yards away. Suddenly he spurred his horse on frantically. He reined slightly right, over the crest of the timbered ridge and straight down through the heavy timber toward the wagons and the blue-clad troops on the valley floor.

Branches of trees clawed at him, sometimes almost brushing him from the saddle. They scratched his face and tore his clothes, but he didn't feel them. He leaned forward, low over the horse's neck so he would be a smaller target.

Dave was aware that he had never in his life ridden in a race as important as this one. He did not delude himself that the Utes wouldn't shoot to kill him. They would kill him as quickly as they would kill any other white.

An arrow tore into his shirt, scratching the muscles of his back and catching itself in the cloth of his shirt. A bullet stung the hindquarters of the horse, making him squeal with pain and run even faster than before.

Dave was halfway to the bottom of the slope by now. Ahead, through a break in the trees, he saw a number of braves in his path intent on stopping him. Beyond he saw Thornburgh's men standing beside their wagons pouring a concentrated fire into the massed Utes. They were trying to open a path for him as desperately as the Utes were trying to block his way.

The braves stood firm until he had almost reached them, but the concentrated fire from the troops was too deadly and too accurate. One after another of the Utes' ponies went thrashing to the ground. Two of the Indians had been hit. One lay motionless in the long dry grass, and the other was crawling away deeper into the timber. The rest broke for the cover of the trees.

Dave drummed his heels more rapidly on the horse's sides. Turning, he slashed the bay's hindquarters with the ends of the reins. The animal gave one last, gallant burst of speed. Leaping over clumps of brush, washouts, and rocks, he thundered toward the troops, with Dave clinging to his back like a cocklebur.

A bullet threw up a puff of dust from a rock beside him, and then whined away as it ricocheted into space. Another bullet struck the bay, entering his body at the right flank and driving forward and toward the left.

The horse stumbled, his head went down, and he somersaulted forward violently, throwing Dave clear twenty feet ahead. He rolled like a ball, half unconscious from the fall. The instant he stopped rolling he scrambled to his feet, shook his head to clear it, and got his bearings. He sprinted toward the blue lines of soldiers less than fifty feet away. They opened a hole in their ranks for him to plunge through. Then he was safe, exhausted, trembling violently, and out of breath, but mercifully alive and relatively unhurt.

CHAPTER
THIRTEEN

Tono listened to the hoofbeats as Dave raced away toward the north. Tono hoped his face had not given away his feelings. He was scared, but he had not wanted Dave to know. Badger was a grown man, and a very strong one. He was as old as Tono's uncle and had considerable power in the tribe. He had the reputation of being a mighty hunter, having once fought and killed a black bear with only his bare hands and a knife.

Tono's hands, holding the rifle, were trembling. He gripped the gun more tightly. Badger moved slightly and Tono said quickly, "Don't move. I don't want to shoot you, but I will."

Badger remained quiet after that. Tono could see that the pulse in his temple was pounding, and his body had an unusual tenseness. Tono recognized the signs of rage and wished he were a thousand miles from here. When he released Badger . . .

He didn't even want to think about it, and yet he didn't regret what he had done. He would do it again, not only because Dave was his friend, but also because what he had done was right.

Dave had not hurt the Utes. He was in no way responsible for what had happened, no more responsible for the whites than Tono was for the Indians. He simply had not deserved to die for Meeker's stubbornness.

Now Tono was aware that it was almost time to begin paying for what he had done. He accepted the possibility that Badger might kill him as soon as he got his rifle back. He also accepted the certainty that he had disgraced his uncle and his family. The Utes might cast Tono out of the tribe. They might want nothing more to do with him.

The wind rustled softly in the leaves of the cottonwoods. The two horses occasionally cracked a twig as they grazed beneath the trees. The sun was warm as it beat down on them, and a dry, dusty smell was in the air.

Tono wondered how all this was going to end. He knew Jack had threatened to attack Thornburgh's troops if they crossed the Milk Creek reservation boundary. He realized that if war erupted between the Indians and the soldiers, all the whites at the agency would almost certainly die.

Tono also knew how awesome was the power of the white men. Their lands stretched east two thousand miles, west for a thousand more. They had a hundred soldiers for every Ute brave.

Tono knew something else: the whites wanted the White River Reservation for themselves. They would use a Ute war as an excuse for seizing it. No matter what happened, even if the Utes defeated Thornburgh's men and wiped them out, they still couldn't win. They would be hunted down like rats, killed or imprisoned.

They would be herded west into the Utah wastelands, or moved to Indian Territory, to land the whites didn't want. Even if they won, the Utes would lose.

They should have listened to Meeker, Tono realized. Instead of fighting him, they should have tried to do what he said. He had only wanted them to raise cattle instead of horses, to cut down trees and saw them into boards for building houses. He had wanted them to plant crops, so that when winter came they could eat and stay alive without the white men's help. But Jack and Colorow and the rest of the chiefs had refused to listen.

He started violently as Badger said, "How long do you think you're going to hold me here?"

"Until he's far enough away so you can't follow and catch up with him," Tono answered.

"He has gone that far now," Badger said. "He has a lead of at least five miles."

"We'll wait a little longer."

"I'll kill you when I get my gun."

"You can try," Tono said.

They waited in silence, the time dragging for Tono. He wasn't sure when it would be safe to release Badger, so he kept him longer than necessary. Finally he stepped back and lowered his gun. He said, "You can go get your rifle now. You can't catch him. If you had believed what he told you, I would not have done what I did."

Badger got to his feet. He glowered at Tono, and Tono wondered what he was going to do. Surprisingly, he did nothing. He mounted his horse and rode north to pick up his rifle.

Tono remained where he was. Badger was gone about twenty minutes. When he returned, he was carrying his rifle. Tono swung to the back of his horse and silently followed Badger south toward White River.

Tono didn't know what his punishment was going to be, but it would be severe. He might be driven from the land he had known and loved. He dreaded to see the look in his uncle's eyes when he learned what his nephew had done. He would not have any friends among the Utes, and now he didn't even have Dave.

They rode swiftly along the dusty two-track road. They had almost reached the river when Tono heard the pounding of horses' hooves coming up behind them. Badger reined his horse to a stop and motioned for Tono to do the same. They waited silently beside the road.

A moment later two Ute braves appeared at the crest of the nearest ridge. One wore a cavalry trooper's hat perched squarely atop his braids. As they hauled their lathered horses to a halt, one of them yelled at Badger, "We have attacked the soldiers at Milk Creek. We have killed their horses and now we are killing them. I bring the word to the villages."

Badger nodded and the two braves rode on. They disappeared a few minutes later over the top of the next ridge to the south. Badger and Tono followed at a steady lope. They crested the last ridge and started down into the wide White River valley. Tono was relieved to see the agency buildings standing, apparently untouched. He could see several of the employees working on a new building. Two of them were on the roof spreading dirt that two others were throwing up to them. He saw a woman come from the boardinghouse, dump a pan of water, and go back inside. The two little Price children were playing in front of the boardinghouse. A small Indian boy darted out through the boardinghouse door and ran like a rabbit to disappear in the brush along the riverbank.

Tono saw a dozen or more Ute braves lounging in the shade beside Meeker's house. Suddenly he felt uneasy as he noticed that all these warriors had rifles.

Badger rode his horse at a steady lope down the road. Tono now glanced at the villages and saw the commotion as the messengers rode in shouting their news that the soldiers had been attacked.

Tono thought, "I have made myself an outcast from the tribe. There is nothing more they can do to me for warning Meeker that Thornburgh's men have been attacked. He will surely be next if I do not."

At the foot of the ridge Badger turned his horse off the road toward the villages. Tono stayed on the road and headed for the agency. He dug into his horse's side with his heels and belabored the horse's hindquarters with his rifle barrel. The animal broke into a hard run, ears laid back.

Tono heard Badger's shouts from behind him. Ahead, he saw a couple of Utes racing toward the agency. They were perhaps a quarter of a mile ahead of him. The two were carrying news of the attack, he realized. Not to Meeker, but to the Indians lounging around the agency.

Tono could not reach Meeker before the two Utes broke the news to the other Indians, but he might get to the agency before they attacked the agent and the rest of the white men. He didn't really believe he could, but there was a chance.

He felt like a traitor. He felt as though he were betraying his Indian heritage, his Indian friends. But he also realized he could do nothing else. Meeker and the other helpless whites at the agency would be attacked and killed. They would be dead within minutes if he was unable to warn them in time.

The two hard-riding braves ahead of him reached the dozen who were lounging in the shade. Tono heard them yell. The Indians leaped to their feet. With horror he saw them suddenly whirl and point their rifles at the white men on the roof of the new building.

Tono opened his mouth to shout a warning, but he made no sound, knowing that shouting was useless now. The slim chance he'd had of saving the white men was gone. He watched smoke puff from the muzzles of the Indians' rifles. He heard the reports and heard their echoes roll back from the ridges on the north. The men fell from the roof. William Post was next. Then Shad Price dropped his shovel and staggered toward the boardinghouse, clutching his belly with both hands.

Flora Ellen Price snatched up her screaming little girl, May, and ran toward her bedroom in the boardinghouse. Frank Dresser lunged after her, carrying a rifle that he had picked up somewhere.

111

Josie grabbed little Johnnie Price and followed them. Smoke puffed from one of the open windows a moment later, but Tono could not see that any of the Utes were hit. He saw a plume of wood smoke rise from the south side of the boarding-house. Soon the dry wood caught and flames leaped high into the still, hot afternoon air.

Helplessly, Tono hauled his horse to a plunging halt. He had been too late to stop the awful things that were happening. He knew, with sudden sharp insight, that in the end the Utes would pay a very high price for this moment of bloody, passionate revenge.

Tono saw Dresser, still carrying the rifle, run from the boardinghouse, followed by Josie and Arvilla Meeker, and by Flora Ellen carrying Johnnie and little May. They disappeared into the small adobe milk house across from the boardinghouse. Dresser was limping, probably wounded in the foot or leg, Tono thought. The door of the milk house slammed shut.

Firing broke out from the direction of Meeker's house. Tono saw several Utes enter the agent's front door. A moment later he heard gunfire from inside the house.

The boardinghouse was a mass of flames on one side. It poured a huge column of smoke a hundred feet into the air. The burning wood made sounds like pistol shots.

Other buildings were burning now. The Utes were systematically destroying the hated structures that represented Meeker's stubbornness, that meant plowing, school for their children, a ban on horse racing, and enforced work for men who had traditionally never

112

worked, who had only made war and hunted wild game.

Afterward the Utes might flee south across the great Roan Plateau. Perhaps they would reach Grand River. They might even go on south as far as the San Juan Mountains and join up with Ouray's band. But Tono knew that the retribution of the whites would follow until payment had been exacted for these murders here.

At least Dave was safe and still alive. Then an awful thought occurred to Tono. The fight between the Utes and the soldiers had already started when Dave left him to ride north. Dave might have been killed; he might have been one of the first to die.

Tono realized that more than likely he would never know. Because he was one of the Utes, he would have to bear his share of the responsibility for what was happening here at the agency. The whites never singled out individuals to prosecute for crimes. They took their vengeance upon the first Indians they caught.

Numb with horror, Tono could only watch the destruction of the White River Agency. He could only turn cold inside as he waited for the Utes to break down the door of the milk house and drag out the screaming women.

CHAPTER
FOURTEEN

Dave sat up and looked around. Half a dozen soldiers were around him, all asking questions at once. How were the workers at the agency? Was Meeker still alive? Were the women safe? When Charlie Lowry and Henry Jim had returned from the agency, they had reported that all was well, but that had been two days ago.

Dave nodded vigorously to all the questions. He got to his feet, drawing the letter Meeker had given him from his pocket. He said, "I have a message for Major Thornburgh."

A grizzled sergeant shook his head. "The major's dead. Captain Payne is in command."

"Then I'll give the letter to him."

The sergeant led him away. Dave glanced around. Wagons had been drawn into the shape of a horseshoe, the open end facing the stream, which was about 150 yards away. To fill this gap, horses and mules had been shot, and behind the bulwark formed by their bodies men were frantically digging shallow trenches in the ground.

Dave realized with horror that the soldiers had been beaten badly by the Indians. Now they were on the defensive, without mobility because most of their horses and mules were dead.

He remembered Custer's last stand in Montana three years ago and wondered if this was to be another defeat as bloody and total as that. He and the sergeant reached an officer, and the sergeant said, "Captain, this boy just rode through the Indian lines from the agency. He said he has a message for the major, but I told him the major was dead."

Captain Payne turned his head to look at Dave. His face was red and dusty. A little rivulet of sweat ran down one side of his face. He was tense, his expression very grave, but he seemed calm enough. Dave handed him the letter. Captain Payne tore the envelope open, took out the folded sheet of paper, and read the message hastily.

"Are the agency people all right?" he asked.

"Yes, sir. They were when I left."

"And when was that?"

"Early this morning, sir."

"How did you get through?"

"My friend Tono and an Indian named Badger came most of the way with me. Badger didn't want me to get to you with the message, but Tono held Badger at gunpoint while I got away."

Payne nodded, studying Dave approvingly. "Well, you can't go back. You'll have to stay with us. You can take your choice of duty, I suppose. You can help the cooks, help with the wounded, or take your place in the trenches. I think we can find an extra rifle for you."

"I'll take the rifle, sir."

Dave didn't know whether he could shoot an Indian or not. He supposed he could if it was a choice between shooting Utes or getting shot himself. Payne nodded at the sergeant, who led Dave to one of the wagons. He gave Dave a rifle and a handful of shells and began to show him how to load the gun.

"I have a rifle of my own I use to hunt," Dave said.

The sergeant nodded and walked away. Dave crawled beneath one of the wagons into position between two soldiers, facing south. The men were firing steadily, but as far as Dave could see they weren't hitting anything. Occasionally a bullet would *chunk* into the wagon over their heads, and once a bullet showered splinters down on them.

It was comforting to have two tough, bearded soldiers for company. Dave stared toward the stream, thinking uneasily that the wagons should have been closer to water. One hundred and fifty yards was a long way to go for water when hundreds of Utes were shooting at you.

He could see an ox train halted farther upstream. Most of the oxen had been shot in their yokes. One of them was still struggling, occasionally bawling piteously.

A breeze stirred in the south, moving the long grass on the slope in front of Dave. One of the soldiers beside Dave growled, "Hope them redskins don't get the idea of burnin' off the grass. They'll make it mighty hot for us if they do."

As though the Indians had heard the suggestion, a wisp of smoke suddenly came drifting by. Dave heard a shout behind him and turned his head. Captain Payne was staring south and yelling for Sergeant Poppe. The smoke thickened rapidly, until Dave's eyes were smarting and tears were running down his cheeks. He began to cough almost uncontrollably.

Captain Payne was yelling at the men, "Get blankets and soak them with whatever water can be spared. Be ready to beat out the flames when they get to us." He yelled at Sergeant Poppe, "Sergeant, crawl out there and see if you can't set some backfires. That wall of fire is eight or ten feet high. It'll roast us alive, besides burning up the wagons and running off whatever stock we've got left."

Crouching low, Poppe ran between two of the wagons straight into the smoke. Fortunately for him, the smoke was almost thick enough to hide him from the Indians. A few saw him and fired, but he disappeared into the drifting smoke, apparently still unhurt.

Dave watched anxiously for signs of the backfires. He didn't see what good they were going to do out where Poppe had disappeared. By the time they got here, they'd be raging as fiercely as the original fire.

He turned his head toward one of the soldiers at his side. "Hadn't we ought to burn the grass right in front of us? Wouldn't that keep the fires from getting too close to us?"

The man looked at him and then at the man on the other side of Dave. He said, "The kid's right, Mac. Got any matches?"

"Sure." The man took a handful of wooden matches from his pocket and passed some to Dave, who handed part of them on to the other man. The first man said, "Let's go. I'd rather get shot than burned to death."

Dave and the two soldiers leaped to their feet. Crouching low, the three ran half a dozen yards forward. By now the smoke was a pall over the beleaguered men. Dave knelt and scratched a match on the sole of his shoe. He lighted the grass, then moved quickly a yard to his right and lighted it again. It flared up furiously. Dave lighted two more fires, expecting at any moment to feel a bullet thud into him. Then he got up and sprinted for the wagon.

He reached it about twenty feet ahead of the fires he and the others had set. He dived beneath it and raised his head to look. The two soldiers who had been with him under the wagon dived back beneath it, raising a cloud of dust. Dave could see others all along the line following their example, setting fires close to the wagons so that the grass for a dozen yards out would be burned before the main fire reached them.

"That doggone wind," one of the men beside Dave said worriedly. "If it doesn't let up, we'll be roasted for sure."

All three were now choking and coughing uncontrollably. Dave's eyes were streaming tears. He wondered if the smoke was a screen to hide the approach of the Indians. If it was, they would come screaming through it to attack the troops as soon as the fire had passed.

He gripped his rifle so tightly that his knuckles turned white, trying to see in spite of his streaming

118

eyes. He tried to hold his breath so that he wouldn't inhale any more smoke, but he was unable to do that for more than a minute at a time. When he did breathe again it was worse than before and started the agony of coughing all over again.

Sergeant Poppe came racing back, his clothes afire, having been caught between the main fire and his own backfire. He reached the wagons at the same time as the first backfire, the one started by Dave and the others, reached the beleaguered camp. He threw himself to the ground and rolled over and over. Dave and another trooper crawled out from beneath the wagon to help beat out the flames in his clothing with their hands.

The first backfire crawled under the wagons and beyond into the camp itself, and for several minutes the men were busy beating out the flames with whatever came to hand, sometimes even scattering them with their feet because there was nothing else.

The smoke was now so thick Dave couldn't see the far side of the defense perimeter. He thought it was a good thing it was thick, else the Indians would be killing the troopers like flies. As it was, the firing had almost stopped as the Indians waited for the smoke to clear away.

Dave's hands were burned from beating out the flames in Poppe's clothes. His hair and eyebrows were singed. His face was black from smoke and soot, and blistered in places from the heat. He had found an old gunnysack and was beating out grass fires within the perimeter as fast as he could.

He heard a shout, "Here it comes!" and turned to look. The main wall of fire was just now reaching the place, half a dozen yards beyond the wagons, where the backfires had been set. It was taller than a man, yellow and crackling, and the heat was unbelievable. Dave saw the canvas top of the wagon catch fire and ran to climb up on the wagon seat. With his smoking gunnysack he beat at the flames, extinguishing them, and then beat out the glowing embers one by one.

All along the line men were similarly occupied, working silently, grimly, knowing that if the wagons burned there would be nothing left to protect them from the bullets of the Indians. The roar of the wall of flame was almost deafening.

Horses trumpeted with terror and men ran to keep them from running away. An ammunition wagon caught fire and a line of men formed to pass the ammunition to safety despite the danger that it might explode.

Each man did what needed to be done. No orders were given — indeed, if they had been given they could not have been heard. Out beyond the wagons the wall of flame slowly died for lack of fuel. But the heat and smoke continued unabated and the horses reared and fought at the picket line, screaming in terror and trying to pull away.

Dave crawled back beneath the wagon. He recovered his rifle and uncovered his cartridges, which he had covered with dirt to protect them from the flames. The Indians might come riding through the smoke now at any time, and the troopers had better be ready when they did.

The fire rolled over the ox train. No backfires had been built in front of it and no one was there to fight the flames. The wagons caught and blazed high, and John Gordon, the freighter, growled, "There goes them red flannel shirts Meeker ordered for his blasted Indians."

Behind the beleaguered troops, the fire now swept crackling up the valley, leaving a blackened, desolate landscape in its wake. Ahead of Dave, everything was black, still smoldering. Here and there a clump of sagebrush burned sluggishly or a piñon pine burned vigorously, sending up a thick column of black, oily smoke.

He still coughed occasionally from the thin smoke blowing over them, but no Indians came screaming down on them. Perhaps they had seen their plan fail when the backfires were built. By the time the ground had cooled enough for them to ride across, the soldiers were ready for the charge. It occurred to Dave that the Indians had lost their best opportunity for complete victory.

Some random sniping continued as the afternoon wore away. Captain Payne took advantage of a lull in the firing to order the dead men buried temporarily in the animal breast-works. There were ten altogether, and one of them was Charlie Lowry, whom Dave had liked.

The burying had barely been completed when Joe Rankin, one of the scouts, walked to the captain and pointed toward the south. Smoke was rising in the far distance, visible now because the smoke of the grass fire was blowing away on a stiff crosswind.

"Are they firing the timber?" Payne asked.

Rankin shook his head. "It ain't likely. They wouldn't set no fires on their own reservation, captain. No, sir. It's my guess that smoke is from the buildings at the agency burning. That's right where they are."

"Couldn't it be haystacks, Joe?"

Rankin shrugged. "Could be, I suppose. But I don't think it is."

Dave felt the cold hand of dread slip along his spine. If the buildings of the agency were afire, it probably meant the people at the agency were dead. He thought with horror of the two little Price children, Johnnie and May, and of the women, Flora Ellen, Josie, and Mrs. Meeker.

Then he thought of Frank, who seemed younger than he was and had been so easily frightened on guard that night. He thought of big Shad, who had let Dave work with him when the waiting had become intolerable. He guessed he had known all the time it would end this way, and still he had hoped it could be averted.

Rankin and Captain Payne stood beside the wagon under which Dave and the two soldiers lay. The captain's voice was lowered so no one else could hear. Apparently he did not realize that Dave and the two men were so close.

"We're in trouble, Joe," Payne said. "The Indians can live off the meat of Gordon's oxen for days and we're short of food. A third of our men are either wounded or

122

dead. By Thursday we'll be out of food and we've got to have water tonight, so I guess there's only one thing that can be done. As soon as it's dark, somebody's got to get through the Indian lines, ride to Rawlins, and bring a relief force back."

"I reckon that means me," Rankin said.

"You or John Gordon," Payne said. "You're the only two men who know the country well enough to have a chance of getting through."

Rankin said without the least hesitation, "All right, captain. I'll go to Rawlins. Send Gordon to Middle Park after Captain Dodge. He knows the country east of here a lot better than I do."

"I'll go talk to Gordon," Payne said, "and I'll find a couple of troopers to go with you."

Dave saw Payne stride away. Rankin remained beside the wagon. The captain was gone a few minutes. When he returned, Gordon and two troopers were with him.

"I've been thinking about it, captain," Rankin said. "And I've got a plan. You say you need water. Why don't you send us out with a water detail? We can go with them as far as the agency road, and there we'll leave 'em and make a run for it. If any Injuns try to stop us, Gordon and I can take to the brush while these two men fight a delaying action. That'll give us time to get clear and then these two can retreat back to the water detail."

Payne was silent for a time, probably considering what Rankin had said, Dave thought. Then the captain said, "All right, Joe. That sounds like a damn good plan."

They moved away, and when they were gone one of the men lying beside Dave growled, "Don't sound to me like we got much chance."

"This is what we signed up for," the other man said in resignation. "Nobody told us we wasn't gonna have a fight. I only wish we wasn't pinned down this way. I'd like to show them red devils a thing or two."

Dave didn't say anything. The soldiers didn't know what had caused the trouble at the agency and he knew they didn't care, so he didn't offer to tell them.

He closed his eyes. They still smarted from the smoke. Now and then, smoke from the smoldering clumps of brush and trees drifted toward them and his eyes would start watering again. He lay there, thinking that Meeker had saved his life by sending him here with the message for Thornburgh. Tono had saved it again back on the road by risking his own life to hold Badger while he got away.

Meeker was probably dead by now. Tono might be, too. How could you repay dead men? Dave pondered this, but no amount of thinking brought any satisfactory answer to the gloomy question.

A sergeant began moving around the compound assigning men to the water detail that would move out after dark. One of the men beneath the wagon volunteered and, before he realized what he was doing, Dave spoke up and volunteered, too.

Rankin and John Gordon began to saddle their horses and fill their saddlebags with food and cartridges. Rankin tied a sack of oats for his horse behind his saddle, along with the sack of food.

The sun was down now and gray was creeping slowly across the sky. In the last thin light, the Utes came, charging the soldiers' position recklessly.

Captain Payne yelled, "Hold your fire until they're close. Easy now, men. Make every bullet count."

A few shots cracked out, but most of the men followed the captain's orders and held their fire until the Indians were less than a hundred yards away. Suddenly a ragged volley rolled out along the line of bulwarks and redoubts. Clouds of bluish powder smoke billowed out in front of the men.

The toll among the Utes was terrible. The first volley toppled a dozen from their saddles. The horses veered aside and galloped away riderless. The second volley roared out, as ragged as the first and as deadly for the Indians. Twelve or fifteen braves were knocked out of their saddles. They lay sprawled with the others on the black, burned-over ground.

What remained of the attacking force withdrew. Several wounded Indians crawled away. The sky darkened rapidly. Dave had been sure he could not shoot at the Indians, but he had. Now he got up and, with the other trooper who had volunteered, went to where the water detail was gathering. He heard Payne call, "Are you ready, Joe?"

"Ready, captain."

Quietly the water detail, loaded with canteens and accompanied by Rankin and Gordon, slipped out of the circle of wagons and dead horses and headed toward the creek.

Dave had no idea what lay ahead of them. He found himself wishing he had kept his mouth shut and not volunteered. But he had, and he'd just as well make the best of it.

They were halfway to the trees that lined the creek, and Dave could hear the sound of running water. Toward the south, he could see the cook fires of the Utes and sometimes could see an Indian pass in front of one of them.

Rankin and Gordon, leading their horses, walked behind the detail. One of the horses stepped on a branch and broke it with a sound like a pistol shot. Rankin murmured, "Look sharp, boys."

Suddenly there was a loud crashing of brush ahead, and an instant later a rifle flared in the darkness. Rankin said, "Run for it, boys. I think there's only one of them, and the wounded sure need the water."

The men ahead of Dave broke into a run. The rifle flared again, this time to be answered immediately by Rankin's pistol. There was a cry of pain followed by a crash and a groan.

The detail was trotting straight toward the Indian Rankin had shot. Dave thought he might only be wounded and therefore doubly dangerous. As they reached the creek, Rankin said, "So long, boys. Get your water fast and get on back. Them shots will bring the others as fast as they can get here."

Rankin and Gordon mounted and their horses thundered away. The soldier with Dave said urgently, "Fill the canteens, kid. I'll keep an eye out for the Indians."

Dave hurried to the edge of the stream. He knelt, uncorked the dozen canteens he was carrying, and held them under water, two at a time, until they stopped gurgling. He had laid his rifle beside him and once he felt for it, needing the reassurance of its hard, cold steel.

Others knelt on both sides of him. After each canteen was filled, Dave corked it and slung it across his back. It seemed to be an endless task, particularly since they all knew the Utes were on their way to investigate the shots.

The darkness was oppressive, and Dave kept thinking that the gurgling of the stream might hide the sounds of approaching Indians. His hands and knees began to shake. He sighed with relief as he finished filling his canteens and stood up, heavily burdened by their weight. The trooper next to him said, "All right, you watch now while I fill mine." He knelt beside the stream and began filling his canteens.

No one was talking. All seemed to be holding their breath. Dave faced toward the Indian fires, straining his eyes and ears, wishing desperately that the troopers filling canteens would hurry so they could get back.

Suddenly, not a dozen yards away, a shadow crossed between Dave and one of the Indian fires. He flung the rifle to his shoulder and waited an instant until the shadow crossed the fire again. He fired instantly and was rewarded by a high yell of pain.

Behind Dave, the troopers struggled to their feet. Others whose canteens were filled opened fire, too. Indians hidden in the trees fired back.

A man yelled, "That's enough! Let's get back with what we've got!"

Keeping close together, the men ran back toward the fortified position they had left only a few minutes before. The canteens rattled and thumped against their legs. Some, less heavily loaded, stayed in the rear, occasionally firing at the Indians in the trees.

One of Dave's canteens was hit. The bullet made a dull thud and the water ran out and drenched his leg. A man was hit and he cursed steadily all the way back.

The wagons looming up ahead were the most welcome sight Dave had ever seen. A moment later, they were safely inside the perimeter. Then the troopers waiting behind the wagons poured such a heavy fusillade into the trees that the Indians retreated out of rifle range.

Dave dropped the canteens he was carrying and, out of breath, sank down to the ground. He couldn't help thinking about the close call he'd had. If the bullet that had hit the canteen had been a little farther to the left . . . he shook his head, wondering if any of them were going to get out of this alive.

CHAPTER
FIFTEEN

Tuesday was hot and dry. Some of the Indians had apparently withdrawn, but those who remained kept up a steady, sniping rifle fire throughout the day.

The dead horses within the makeshift fort began to swell as the hot sun beat down upon them. Unshaven, grimy soldiers stared listlessly over the breastworks. Dave heard a corporal growl, "Give these carcasses another day under this hot sun and we won't be able to stand 'em. By the time a relief force gets here, we'll be dead from smellin' the stink."

It was obvious that Payne and his officers were concerned about the problem, but there was nothing they could do. The one bright spot was the fact that they no longer had to worry about fire. The grass and brush that had surrounded the tiny fort were gone. There was simply nothing left for the Utes to burn.

After eating, Dave sprawled beneath the wagon and stared at the green timbered hillsides where the Utes kept watch. He seldom saw any of them, but he knew they were there. The sporadic rifle fire was proof of that.

He looked at the blackened expanse of valley, where nothing moved. He looked south, where the smoke had been yesterday, but he saw no smoke today. The agency buildings were gone, he supposed, burned to the ground. Buildings that had been erected at considerable expense for the Utes had been burned by them.

Several times he wondered what had happened to Tono. He hoped that Badger had not killed his friend, or hurt him seriously, yet he knew that Tono had probably been punished.

This question seemed to turn up in his mind every five minutes. Then he wondered how soon a relief force could arrive. Captain Dodge and his troop of black cavalry were in Middle Park. If Gordon had reached them, they could probably get here by the end of the week.

But a force from Rawlins would take longer. It would have to be assembled first, probably at Fort D. A. Russell near Cheyenne, brought to Rawlins by rail, and then marched south to Milk Creek. Dave couldn't even guess how long it would take, and none of the soldiers he asked would venture an opinion.

By Wednesday the stench inside the little compound was almost unbearable. Dave soaked his bandanna and tied it around his face, but it only helped a little. Nobody ate much that day, and sleeping was almost impossible that night. Mercifully, a breeze sprang up. Blowing across the circle, it carried the smell away temporarily.

Even with his face turned into the fresh, cool breeze, Dave still smelled the rotting carcasses. He supposed his nose would remember the stink for weeks, and then he began to wonder if he would ever get rid of it.

On Thursday morning Dave was tense with an expectancy he could not understand. Then, out of the graying semi-darkness beyond the breastworks, he heard a man call softly. He recognized the voice as that of the wagon master, John Gordon, who had ridden to Middle Park for Captain Dodge.

The sentries told Gordon to come on in. A moment later, he slipped into the compound, grimy and unshaven, but as welcome a sight as any of the men had seen for days.

"Dodge is out there with his colored troopers," Gordon told Captain Payne. "He sent me in so you'd cover for 'em when they rode in at dawn."

Quietly, the noncoms went around waking the men who were still asleep. Rifles were readied, along with extra ammunition for them. The men stared out across the graying valley floor, waiting.

The sun touched a few high clouds with salmon pink. And then, sweeter than any sound Dave had ever heard before, came the clear, strong notes of a bugle drifting across the valley.

The bugle call had scarcely stopped when Dave felt muffled vibrations in the ground. Then he saw the troopers of Captain Dodge's company galloping down the valley from the north, spread out in a line, guidons whipping out stiffly in the wind.

The sun tipped up over the nearest eastern hill as they galloped along a quarter of a mile away. The sharp morning light touched their guidons first, and then the blue of their uniforms, and lastly their horses, brown, bay, and black.

The Utes began to fire frantically. Guns cracked on all sides of the little compound. Bullets kicked up dust in front of Dodge's galloping line. A horse went down, somersaulting. The trooper riding him rolled clear, leaped to his feet, and swung up behind one of his comrades who slowed and gave him a stirrup with which to mount.

Dave stared, holding his breath, stirred as he had never been stirred before. There was something beautiful and gallant about that line of blue-clad cavalrymen galloping along in the early sunlight.

Moments later they were leaping over the breastworks and dismounting inside the little fort, grinning, black-faced troopers. Even the wounded raised up from their blankets and cheered hoarsely.

The arrival of Captain Dodge's company didn't seem to worry the Indians. They did not withdraw, so it remained impossible for the troops to leave their little fortified compound. The newcomers helped insure their survival by strengthening the garrison, but they were too few to drive away the besieging Indians.

So the black cavalrymen joined the line of grim-faced, bearded soldiers at the compound's perimeter. They smelled the cloying stench of dead horses; they listened to the groans of the wounded. They watched the puffs of smoke from the muzzles of the Indians' rifles on the hills, and they heard the chunk of bullets hitting the breastworks.

Now they all waited glumly for the relief force from Rawlins that would be strong enough to drive the Indians away. The waiting dragged on through the rest of Thursday, Friday, and Saturday. Each hour's passing reduced the troopers' hopes that rescue would come in time.

The exhausted, hungry men often turned their faces toward the north and listened for the sound of the relief force. A thousand times the question was asked of Gordon, "Do you think Joe Rankin got away?"

Gordon would reply patiently, "I think so, soldier. I think he did. I'd have heard the racket if he'd run into trouble."

"Then where is the relief force? They've had time to get here, haven't they?"

Dave knew he was as bad as the soldiers. He had no notion of time. It seemed a month since he had ridden through the timber to the little fort with the note from Meeker; each of the six days under siege had been so much more than a day. An eternity was a better word, yet he knew that Gordon was right in his answers.

"Maybe they've had time," Gordon would say. "Maybe not. It's a hundred and seventy miles to Rawlins from here. It must have taken Joe at least two nights and a day to cover it. He could send a telegram from Rawlins asking for more troops, but there ain't any more troops at Fort Steele, so they've got to get 'em from someplace else. Fort D. A. Russell, maybe. You've got to sit tight, soldier. They'll get here sure enough. All we can do is wait."

"Yeah. Wait. All we got to do is wait," the trooper would grumble.

So Dave waited along with the rest. He slept as much as possible, because it made the hours pass and it helped him to forget the ever present stench. There had been no more attacks by the Indians, but they were still out there on the hills. Their fire was steady enough to keep the soldiers down.

He dreamed wild and troubled dreams. Sometimes he would see Meeker lying with an arrow in his chest; or the buildings at the agency in flames; or young Frank Dresser running through the sagebrush for his life. There were quiet dreams, too, of his life in Greeley. Dave no longer thought that Greeley was the worst place in the world in which to live.

On Sunday morning he awoke to the brassy, clear notes of a bugle sounding the charge. At first he thought he was dreaming again. For the last day or two he'd had trouble distinguishing between what was a dream and what was real. But as he leaped to his feet and stared into the gray of early dawn, he knew this was no dream. He saw a column of cavalry galloping toward their fort. There were at least four companies.

Behind the cavalry came a column of infantry, and behind the infantry he saw a line of wagons that extended back until it disappeared around a bend in the valley. It must be the biggest army in the world, he thought. He leaned against a wagon, weak with the sheer joy. He was going to live, he was going to be all right.

Dave stared toward the south as the relief column surrounded the besieged position. He found himself thinking once more about the people at the agency. The troops of the relief force would be going on, he thought, to rescue Meeker and the others if they were still alive.

Indians were leaving their positions on the slopes. They mounted their ponies on the hilltops out of rifle range and stared down at the soldiers below.

Dave saw one Indian he thought he recognized, though at this distance he wasn't sure. This one looked like Tono. Dave watched as the Indian rode down a long point to a ridgetop and stared for a time at the commotion below him. Dave was sure now that it was Tono. He raised a hand and waved, and the Indian waved back, then turned his horse and rode along the point and disappeared.

"It was Tono," Dave told himself in relief. "He lived through the fight."

Then the ridgetops were empty in the morning sun. The Utes had gone south, Tono with them. Dave knew he would not see his friend again.

Colonel Merritt, in command of the relief force, took charge decisively. He ordered the bodies that had been temporarily buried in the breastworks dug up and reburied near the corral. Then the survivors moved out of the compound where they had spent a long, miserable week and ate a good hot meal upwind from the rotting carcasses.

Merritt ordered clean uniforms issued to the men, and his soldiers stood guard while they bathed and shaved. Merritt's medical staff helped care for the wounded and placed them in ambulance wagons for the return trip to Rawlins.

Dave sought out Captain Payne. He said hesitantly, "I'd like to go back to the agency with Colonel Merritt, sir. My friends are all there and I've got to know if they're all right." Payne began to shake his head. Dave said, "Please, sir. I've just *got* to go back there. And the colonel will let me go if you ask him to."

Payne studied him thoughtfully for a long, long time. At last he nodded. "I guess you'll be all right if you stay with Merritt's men. I'll talk to him." He started to walk away, then turned his head. "Is there any message you'd like me to send your folks?"

"Yes, sir. I'd like them to know that I'm all right."

"I'll see they get your message, Dave."

He waited breathlessly until Captain Payne returned. He relaxed when he saw the captain nod and grin at him. "The colonel said you can go. But he won't be leaving for several days. He intends to camp here until he receives reinforcements from Fort Snelling in Dakota Territory."

Dave thanked him. The prospect of waiting several days before going south to the agency dismayed him, but he knew there was nothing he could do. Colonel Merritt was in command, and he didn't intend to move until his force was strong enough to overwhelmingly defeat the Utes.

CHAPTER
SIXTEEN

For the next few days everything was relatively quiet at the camp on Milk Creek. A couple of shots were fired at the soldiers, but nothing came of it. A white man, Joe Brady, brought Colonel Merritt a message from Chief Ouray at Los Pinos Indian Agency. In it Ouray commanded all Utes to cease hostilities.

Brady told Merritt he had seen and talked to Chief Jack, and, though Jack had not said so directly, he had implied that all the male whites at the White River Agency were dead. Brady believed the women and children were prisoners.

The long-awaited reinforcements finally arrived, six companies of the Seventh Infantry from Fort Snelling in Dakota Territory. On Saturday, October 11, Merritt led his force of nearly nine hundred men down Coal Creek toward the White River Indian Agency.

The guides were Eugene Taylor and Jim Barker. Because he knew both men, Dave was allowed to ride with them and Colonel Merritt at the head of the column. His stomach felt hollow. He could feel tremors in his hands and legs. He was torn by conflicting emotions. He had begged to be allowed to come along, but now he wished he had gone north instead.

Dave didn't want to see what he believed he was going to see when the column reached the agency. Meeker had been his employer, respected even though he was a stubborn, visionary man with whom Dave had often disagreed. The others had been his friends. Shad Price had seemed like an older brother.

He would not let the soldiers see how he felt. The choice of coming with Merritt or going north had been his, so he kept his face straight ahead. The only visible sign of his anxiety was a lack of color in his face.

One of the guides came upon a trail of blood at the old Danforth coal mine. Merritt detached Jim Barker and a detail of soldiers to follow it while the column ground on ahead.

Dave rode beside Barker following the trail. It could be the trail of a gut-shot buck, Barker told him. Dave found himself praying that it was nothing more. He halted in sheer horror when he saw the body of young Frank Dresser. The soldiers also stopped, staring uneasily at the dead boy.

Frank lay peacefully, as though he had died quietly in his sleep. His coat was under his curly head, neatly folded and used as a pillow. His hand rested on his Winchester, which lay on the ground beside him, fully loaded and cocked. He must have escaped from the agency somehow, but had been discovered and shot. He had crawled up here to die.

Frank had grown up mighty fast, Dave thought with a tightness in his throat. He had died a man. Dave got down from his horse and walked past the body, fighting to control his emotions.

There was a message scrawled on one of the mine timbers. Dave called, "He wrote something here."

Barker asked, "What is it, Dave?"

"It says, 'Been here twenty-one hours. All killed at the agency. Send my money to my mother at Greeley.' It's signed 'Frank Dresser.'"

One of the soldiers went for a stretcher and blanket, and Frank's body was wrapped and carried to the road where it was loaded into a wagon. Sober-faced and somehow older than he had been half an hour before, Dave rode on with the others toward the agency, toward the bloody sight he knew awaited them there.

Suddenly he felt a new and strange emotion growing in him. He had seldom felt it before and never with this intensity. It was hatred, hatred for the Utes.

Tono had been his friend and he had thought he understood Tono, but now he wondered. Tono belonged to a race that could savagely butcher helpless people. Frank Dresser had been hardly more than a child, even though he had died like a man.

Dave had tried to understand the Utes. He had sympathized with them because Meeker had tried to force them into his way of doing things. Now Dave decided his sympathy had been misplaced. They were wild and cruel. They were savages. It was easy to understand why white people all over Colorado hated and feared them as they did.

Five miles short of the agency, the column came upon a burned wagon. Nearby were the bodies of the teamster, Carl Goldstein, and his young helper, Julius Moore.

At the Narrows they found the body of Wilmer Eskridge, the agency employee who had been on his way to Greeley for a vacation. He had agreed to carry a message from Thornburgh back to the agency. He had obviously delivered it to Meeker, for he had a reply to Thornburgh in his pocket. He had paid for his devotion to duty with his life.

The column moved on. At last they reached the agency and halted. The men stared in disbelief. The flagpole still stood and the American flag waved in the light breeze. But beneath it was devastation that reflected the Utes' savage hatred of everything Meeker had done and everything he had tried to force them to do.

Tons of flour were scattered everywhere, contrasting sharply with the black, charred embers. Everything that would burn had been burned. What would not burn had been battered and scattered by the Utes in a frenzy of hatred. Farm machinery was smashed, as were the cooking utensils and stoves.

The first body found among the charred and scattered wreckage was that of Arthur Thompson, his gun still clutched in his hand. Close by was the corpse of Shad Price. Next they found William Post with a twenty-five-pound flour sack clutched in his arms. Not far from Post were the bodies of young Fred Shepard, Harry Dresser, and George Eaton. Eaton's face had been chewed away by wolves.

Still farther along, they found the body of Nathan Meeker, a heavy logging chain around his neck. A barrel stave had been jammed down his throat in a final act of defiance and hatred.

Dave dismounted and stood shaking violently, as though he had a chill. He thought for a time he was going to be sick, and fought the feeling angrily. There was no sign of the women, Josie and Mrs. Meeker and Flora Ellen Price, or of the two children, so they must still be alive.

He looked to the southwest, toward the ascending bulk of the great Roan Plateau. The Utes were up there someplace, he thought, perhaps even now looking down at the white soldiers milling around the charred ruins of the agency. He wondered where Tono was. He felt more certain than ever that he would never see his friend again.

Thinking of the Ute boy, he suddenly became aware of one important fact he had overlooked previously. Tono certainly had not taken part in the murders here. Neither had hundreds of other White River Utes. The murders and the destruction at the agency had been committed by a small handful.

Confusedly, Dave stared at the flaming beauty of the hillsides lying east of the agency. Certainly, he thought, all Indians had good reason to hate and distrust the whites. They had been cheated and lied to and slaughtered, but they had not been abused by *all* white people. Only by a small handful of them.

It was the same with the victims here at the agency, only in reverse, Dave thought. A handful of Utes had gone berserk. The fight on Milk Creek was another matter, for that had been a battle between armed braves and soldiers. The Utes knew what had happened on Sand Creek and on the Washita, and it was understandable that they would try to defend their homes and families against what they considered an invading force.

But here at the agency a handful of braves, perhaps lacking courage to stand and fight a column of soldiers, had tasted blood and gone mad. The horrible injustice of it made Dave sick. Frank Dresser had never hurt the Utes. Nor had big, good-natured Shad Price. Their lack of guilt had not saved them, however. They had paid with their lives for what others had done to the Indians.

Dave turned to his horse, thinking that anyone who was different from the great majority of people was made to suffer. He remembered a boy in Greeley who was the victim of many cruel jokes because he stuttered. Another boy who was deaf was called stupid by his playmates.

It was the same with the Indians, who were too few in numbers to protect themselves. Dave stared at the long valley of the White River with its thousands of fertile acres, and knew it would not be long until white men would settle here and plow the land Meeker had tried to plow for the benefit of the Utes. He didn't know where the Utes would be sent, but he was certain they would be moved to land the whites didn't want, along with the other bands of Utes at the Los Pinos Agency who had had no part in this massacre.

Dave's reflective mood was broken by Merritt's orders to pull back from the ruins of the agency. Merritt bivouacked his troops and detailed a burial party. Graves were dug for the slain members of the agency staff and for the teamster Goldstein and his helper.

At sundown, the chaplain read the burial service and, one by one, the bodies, wrapped in army blankets, were lowered into their graves. Dave, standing a few feet behind the chaplain, discovered that he was weeping. He was not the only one. Many of the battle-hardened soldiers were wiping their eyes.

Completely exhausted, Dave slept that night as if he had been drugged. In the morning he stayed with a small detachment at the agency and watched Merritt's column wind its way slowly up the long slopes leading to the Roan Plateau, following the Indians' trail.

A newspaperman who had accompanied Merritt south stood beside Dave, also watching the progress of the troops.

"You're the only one left, aren't you, son?" the reporter asked.

Dave nodded. "I suppose I am, unless the women and the two children are still alive."

"Not much chance of that," the reporter said bitterly. "Not in the hands of those dirty savages."

Dave said quietly, "I think they're still alive. The Utes had great respect for them."

The reporter stared at him. "Respect? From an Indian? Boy, don't make jokes with me." He motioned toward the ruins of the agency. "Not after that. The only good Indian is a dead Indian. And pretty soon there are going to be a lot of good Indians up there on that plateau."

Dave faced the reporter, his eyes flashing angrily. "Indians understand respect. They understand loyalty. Meeker would have been one of the first to tell you that. One of those Indians you're so ready to condemn saved my life at the risk of his own. If he had been a 'good Indian,' as you put it, I would be a dead white."

The reporter was staring at him more closely now. "I heard how you brought that message from Meeker. That took courage, cold, tough courage, and that's a quality I admire." Again he waved a hand toward the gutted buildings of the agency. "But what about all this? And those graves we filled yesterday?"

"The whole Ute tribe didn't do this. It was done by a few."

"You want to forgive them?" the reporter asked incredulously. "After they've killed your friends."

Dave shook his head. "No," he said. "They committed a terrible crime and they should be punished for it. But only the ones who committed the crime should pay. Not all the Indians. But all of them will pay. The ones the soldiers don't kill will be driven off their reservation. You'll see."

Dave turned and walked away, not wanting to talk about it anymore. The reporter stared after him, a puzzled frown on his face.

Dave headed toward the river, realizing how much he had changed since coming to the agency. He was not even the same boy who had delivered the lunch pail to Shad Price. He had been afraid when he carried Meeker's message to Captain Payne, but he had overcome his fears. And he had survived those endless days of fighting and hunger and the stench of rotting carcasses, when hope of rescue seemed very, very slim. He had taken a giant stride toward growing up.

Suddenly Dave knew what he wanted to do when he was old enough. He would work with the Indians, wherever they were when that time came. He wanted to understand them and he wanted them to understand white people. If he were successful, things like the Meeker massacre would never need to happen again.

AUTHORS' NOTE

General Charles Adams, who had at one time been the Indian agent at both the White River and the Los Pinos agencies, was a good friend of a number of the Ute chiefs, including Ouray, who lived near the Los Pinos Agency and in theory was the head chief of all the Utes. After the massacre, Secretary of the Interior Carl Schurz asked Adams to go back into the wilderness and try to rescue the Meeker women, Mrs. Price, and the two children.

Adams organized a party of five whites and thirteen Indians at the Los Pinos Agency and rode down the Uncompahgre River toward the Grand River. When they reached the mouth of Whitewater Creek, two Ute runners arrived with news that Chief Jack's band was furious because Merritt's soldiers were moving south toward their camp. The lives of the five white captives were now in great danger.

At great risk to his life and the lives of the men with him, General Adams moved rapidly into the mountains to the Indian camp where the captives were being held. He secured their release. They were taken to the home of Chief Ouray, near the present-day town of Montrose,

Colorado. There Ouray's wife, Chipeta, made them welcome, and it is said that she cried over them.

Josephine Meeker, impressed by their treatment and by Ouray's home, later wrote, "We found carpets on the floor, curtains at the windows, lamps on the tables, stoves in the rooms, and fires burning. We were given the whole house to ourselves."

After having spent twenty-three days as captives in the lodges of the Utes, Mrs. Meeker, Josephine, Mrs. Price, and her two children journeyed to their former homes in Greeley. The suspense and horror of the last few months were over. Their frightening memories would be dulled by time, and they would go down in history as the only survivors of "The Meeker Massacre."

ABOUT THE AUTHORS

Wayne D. Overholser has written many popular Western novels, including *The Violent Land, Bitter Journey, Cast a Long Shadow,* and *Law Man.* The latter two were made into motion pictures. He has also won two Spur awards from the Western Writers of America. The Overholsers make their home in Boulder, Colorado.

Lewis B. Patten is also a well-known Western novelist. His latest books include *Bones of the Buffalo, Death of a Gunfighter,* and *The Red Sabbath* (which also won a Spur award from the Western Writers of America). Mr. Patten and his family live in Denver, Colorado.

ISIS publish a wide range of books in large print, from fiction to biography. Any suggestions for books you would like to see in large print or audio are always welcome. Please send to the Editorial Department at:

ISIS Publishing Limited
7 Centremead
Osney Mead
Oxford OX2 0ES

A full list of titles is available free of charge from:

Ulverscroft Large Print Books Limited

(UK)
The Green
Bradgate Road, Anstey
Leicester LE7 7FU
Tel: (0116) 236 4325

(Australia)
P.O. Box 314
St Leonards
NSW 1590
Tel: (02) 9436 2622

(USA)
P.O. Box 1230
West Seneca
N.Y. 14224-1230
Tel: (716) 674 4270

(Canada)
P.O. Box 80038
Burlington
Ontario L7L 6B1
Tel: (905) 637 8734

(New Zealand)
P.O. Box 456
Feilding
Tel: (06) 323 6828

Details of **ISIS** complete and unabridged audio books are also available from these offices. Alternatively, contact your local library for details of their collection of **ISIS** large print and unabridged audio books.